ACT OF FAITH AND OTHER STORIES

Act of Faith

AND OTHER STORIES

by IRWIN SHAW

Short Story Index Reprint Series

BOOKS FOR LIBRARIES
A Division of Arno Press, Inc.
New York • 1980

Reprinted 1971 by arrangement with
Random House, Inc.

Special acknowledgment is made to *The New Yorker* magazine in which originally appeared *Preach on the Dusty Roads, Faith at Sea, Night in Algiers, Walking Wounded, Gunners' Passage, The Priest, Act of Faith* and *Hamlets of the World.* Acknowledgment is also due *Collier's Weekly* for *Retreat, Part in a Play* and *Medal from Jerusalem,* and *Accent* for *The Veterans Reflect.*

INTERNATIONAL STANDARD BOOK NUMBER:
0-8369-4024-5

LIBRARY OF CONGRESS CATALOG CARD NUMBER:
70-169561

TO PETER VIERTEL

CONTENTS

ACT OF FAITH AND OTHER STORIES

PREACH ON THE DUSTY ROADS

Nelson Weaver sat at his desk and wrote, "Labor . . . Bridgeport plant . . . $1,435,639.77." Then he put his sharply pointed hard pencil down among the nine other sharply pointed hard pencils arrayed in severe line on the right side of the shining desk, below the silver-framed photograph of his dead wife.

He looked at the leather clock on the back edge of his desk. 10:35. Robert wouldn't be along for ten minutes yet.

Nelson Weaver picked up his pencil and looked at the long sheets of paper, closely covered with typewritten figures, to his right. "Depreciation . . . $3,100,456.25," he wrote.

The tax sheets for Marshall and Co., Valves and Turbines, were nearly done. He had sat at this desk for thirty-five days, working slowly and carefully, from time to time deliberately putting down a number on the page, like Cézanne with his six strokes a day on a water color, until the huge elaborate structure of Marshall and Co.'s finances, which reached from bank to bank and country to country, from Wilmington, Delaware, where it was incorporated, to Chungking, China, where it sold electrical equipment to Chiang Kai-shek; until all this sprawling, complex history of money paid and money gained and credit offered and rejected and profit and loss, palpable and impalpable, was laid bare and comprehensible on five short pages of his clean accountant's figures.

Nelson looked at the leather clock. 10:40. The train was leaving at 11:15. Robert had better hurry.

Nelson looked at the *$3,100,456.25* he had written. For the thousandth time he admired the delicate, tilted, bookkeeper's 2 he had early in his career learned to make. Somehow that 2 was to him a badge of his profession, a sign of his talents, an advertisement of the difficult rare world of figures in which he moved skilfully and at ease, turning sweat and clamor, heat and smoke, bonanza and disaster, into clear, rigid, immutable tables.

10:43. Where was Robert? Nelson got up and went to the window and looked out. He looked down the steel and granite fifty stories to the street. He laughed a little to himself when he realized he was trying to pick his son out of the hurry and confusion of 49th Street five hundred feet below.

He went back to his desk and sat down and picked up the sheet of paper on which he had been working. Tax sheets represented a formal and intricate game in which the players solemnly and conventionally juggled abstractions, like Spinoza proving God, to bring about very real and tangible results, like the great man who, in 1932, proved that J. P. Morgan had no taxable income. Once, in 1936, Nelson, in a rare burst of capriciousness, had made up two tax sheets. One, that Marshall and Co. had actually submitted to the government. And the other, with a change here and there to conform more to the actual realities of iron and sweat rather than the formal accountant's symbolism of numbers and deductible percentages. There had been a difference of $700,962.12. Nelson had carried the second sheet around with him for his private amusement for a week and then burned it, wisely.

This year, with the blossoming expansion of Marshall and

Co. for war orders and the jump in the surplus profits tax, the difference between the real and the formal would be immense, over a million dollars, Nelson figured. Marshall and Co. paid him $40,000 a year. He was quite a bargain, he told himself grimly.

10:47. No Robert yet. Nelson put down the paper because the figures were beginning to jump before his eyes. More and more frequently he found that happening to him. Well, along with the waistline that grew an inch a year and the tendency to wake at five in the morning and his lack of shock at overhearing people calling him a middle-aged gentleman, that had to be expected of a man who had led a quiet, rather unhealthy life at a desk and was now over fifty. . . .

The door opened and Robert came in in his new lieutenant's uniform, with the rawhide suitcase Nelson had given him in his hand.

"On our way, Pop," Robert said. "The U.S. Army is waiting on tiptoe."

They smiled at each other and Nelson took his beautiful gray Homburg out of the closet and put it carefully on before the mirror.

"I was afraid you wouldn't make it," he said, delicately fingering the brim of the hat.

Robert was over at the window, staring out at New York, shining all around in the early summer sun, with the Hudson a flat blue highway against the cliffs of New Jersey and the buildings piled against each other like stiff confectionery in the light morning air. "Lord, Lord . . ." Robert murmured. "What a place to work! You ought to be sitting here writing the Ninth Symphony, Pop."

Nelson smiled at him and took his arm. "I'm not writing the

Ninth Symphony." He would have liked to carry Robert's bag for him to the elevator and even made a move for it, but Robert detected it and switched the bag without a word to the other hand.

There was a pretty, dark-haired woman in a fine, severe black dress that looked on her as black dresses are supposed to look on smart women who work in fashionable businesses, and rarely do. She had her hair swept up for the summer morning and she looked pert and sharp and pretty and grownup all at once, and she looked coolly and approvingly, Nelson noticed, at his tall son, standing beside him, very slender and straight and self-consciously handsome in his new dark-green lieutenant's blouse with the proud gold bar shining on each shoulder.

Robert smiled a little to himself, conscious of the cool approving stare, helplessly and a little ashamedly pleased with himself for provoking it.

"Sometimes," he said, as he and Nelson got out of the elevator and walked toward Fifth Avenue, with the woman lost behind them, "sometimes, Pop, they ought to be allowed to arrest a man for the thoughts that pass through his head."

They grinned at each other and Robert took a deep full breath, looking around him, the smile still on his lips, before he got into the taxicab and said, "Grand Central, please."

They sat quietly as the cab dodged through the streets. Nelson looked steadfastly at the shining rawhide bag. You saw bags like that, he thought, on Friday afternoons in the summertime, on station platforms where people in summer clothes gaily waited for trains going to New England, to the Adirondacks, to Cape Cod . . . Somehow, he felt, to make the picture complete, there should be a tennis racket lying beside it, in its bright rubber case, and a girl's voice, light and excited, dominating the scene, saying swiftly, laughing, "Olive oil and vinegar in equal parts and a few drops of glycerin and just smear yourself, darling, every hour. There was this lifeguard at Hobe Sound and he was out in the sun twelve hours a day and that was all he used and he was as brown as the outside of an old piece of roast beef . . ."

But instead it was Robert's voice saying, "Five medium tanks . . ."

"What was that?" Nelson looked at his son, apologetically. "I'm sorry. I didn't quite . . ."

"When I get back," Robert said, "I'm put in command of five medium tanks. Twelve tons apiece, with a crew of four men. They represent an investment of about three hundred thousand bucks. And I've got to tell them, start, stop, go here, go there, kindly demolish that hot dog stand to the left, would you be so good as to put six shells into that corset and lingerie shop five blocks down the street." He grinned widely. "Me. I never even ran a set of electric trains before in my life. The faith that the U.S. Government has in me! I'm going to develop a beautiful case of stage fright when the time comes for me to look those five medium tanks in the eye."

"You'll do all right," Nelson said soberly.

Robert stared at him seriously for a moment, the smile gone. "I suppose so," he said.

The cab wheeled into Grand Central and they got out.

"We have fifteen minutes," Robert said, looking up at the clock. "How about one quick one, to oil the wheels?"

"Is anyone else seeing you off? Nelson asked, as they walked through the dim, shuffling, echoing vault, toward the bar of the Commodore Hotel. "No girls?"

"Nope," said Robert, smiling. "Can't start that. If you invite one you've got to invite them all. It'd look like a reunion of Vassar graduates, classes of 38 to 41, inclusive." He laughed aloud. "I wouldn't like to make such a showy exit."

Nelson smiled at the joke, but was aware that the joke covered the fact that Robert had saved his final private good-bye before he went to war for his father. He wished there was some way to tell Robert he understood and was grateful, but whatever words he could think of would be clumsy and tragic, so he said nothing. They went into the Commodore and stood at the long bar, quiet now and cool and dim in the eleven o'clock pause before the day's drinking began.

"Two martinis," Robert said to the bartender.

"I haven't had a drink in the morning," Nelson said, "since Arthur Parker's wedding. 1936."

"What the hell," Robert said. "There's a war on."

There was the pleasant sound of the ice clinking in the mixer and the faint strange smell of the gin rising in the empty bar and the pungent tiny smell of the lemon peel that the bartender twisted delicately over the full cold glasses.

They lifted their drinks and Nelson looked past his son's lean, well-loved head, capped and young and martial, with the gold and leather of the United States Army shining on it. Nelson looked along the bar into the dim recesses of the low-ceilinged, long room, as neat and orderly and expectant with its empty and regular tables and chairs as only a bar or restaurant prepared for the day's eating and drinking can be. How many farewells had been said in this room, this drinking place next to the trains that spread out across the whole huge continent. How many final good-byes. How many last kisses between husband and wife. How many gulped and tasteless drinks, how much shock of alcohol to take the first terrible edge off the pain of loss and distance. How many farewelling ghosts sat at those regular tables, their endless irrevocable good-byes echoing among the frivolous glasses. How full the company of grieving leavetakers, each of them tasting death in this snatched last moment over whisky, before the train rolled out. . . .

Nelson looked squarely, steadily at his one child's military head. He raised his glass a little higher, touching his son's glass. "To a quick end of the business," he said.

They drank. The drink tasted powerful and rich and burning and immediately effective against his morning palate. Robert drank with zest, tasting the full savor of the drink happily, rolling it over his tongue. "You'd be surprised," he said, "how hard it is to get a good martini in the Tank Corps."

Nelson watched him drink and remembered a day in the country, three years ago, when Robert was twenty. It was summertime and they were both on vacation and had a house in Vermont and Robert had been out swimming all afternoon and had come in, wet-haired, tan, barefoot, wrapped in a huge white bathrobe, with a faded blue towel swung around his shoulders, summertime printed on his freckled nose and the tan backs of his lake-washed hands . . . He had swung through the screen door, singing loudly, "Stormy weather, since my gal and I ain't together. . . ." He had padded along barefoot, leaving high-arched stains of lakewater on the grass rugs directly to the kitchen. When Nelson had gone into the kitchen, he saw Robert sitting at the porcelain table, still humming "Stormy Weather," with an open bottle of cold beer in one hand, the moisture condensing coolly on the glass, and in the other hand a huge, ludicrous sandwich he had made for himself with two great jagged slices of rye bread and a quarter pound of Swiss cheese and two mountainous slices of cold baked ham and a tremendous cold beefsteak tomato cut in three fat, meaty slices. Robert was sitting there, tilted back in the flimsy kitchen chair, the late afternoon sun shining obliquely on him through the high old-fashioned window, slowly dripping lakewater, the giant of a sandwich and the bottle of beer happily in his hands, his mouth full of cheese and tomato and ham and bread and cold beer, the song somehow working out of his throat in a bumbling joyous monotone. He waved the sandwich airily at Nelson when Nelson appeared at the door.

"Starving," he mumbled. "Swam four miles. Got to keep my energy up."

"You've got to eat dinner in an hour," Nelson said.

Robert grinned through the food. "I'll eat dinner. Let nobody worry." And he took another fabulous bite from the monstrous sandwich.

Nelson watched him eat, smiling a little to himself.

"Want me to make you a sandwich?" Robert asked.

"No, thanks."

"Great maker of sandwiches . . ."

Nelson shook his head, smiling. "I'll wait for dinner." He watched his son eat. The full white teeth shining in the sunburned face, biting strongly and evenly into the food, the lean muscles of the strong throat, rising out of the white bathrobe, moving calmly as he tilted the bottle back and gulped the beer. . . .

"When I was your age," Nelson said, "I ate just like that. . . ."

And suddenly Robert had looked at him very soberly as though seeing his father twenty years old—and loving him—

and seeing the long years that came after with pride and pity . . .

"Well . . ." Robert ate the olive at the bottom of his glass and put the glass down with a little flat tinkle that ran lightly through the quiet bar. "Well, the train's waiting. . . ."

Nelson looked around and shook his head and the Vermont kitchen and the sunburned boy and the bottle of beer beaded with icebox-cold all disappeared. He finished his drink and paid and together he and Robert hurried across the station to the gate where Robert's train was waiting. There was an air of bustle and impatience about the gate, and a soldier and his mother and two female relatives were weeping together in a sodden mass and somehow he and Robert shook hands and there was a last wave and no words because they each knew that any word through the tortured throat would bring with it sobs—and Robert went down the long incline to the dark station below. His rawhide bag gleamed among the descending passengers and he was gone. . . .

Nelson turned and walked slowly toward the street. As he walked he thought of the capped head and the rawhide bag going down the long incline to the waiting train, to the medium tanks, to the waiting guns, the waiting agony, going lightly and zealously and unquestioningly off to war. He remembered, although a little mistily, with the martini and the shuffling steps on the marble floor, and the weeping at the gates of the soldier's women, all serving to blur and confuse and make remote, he remembered watching Robert playing tennis last summer. Robert played very smoothly and well, lanky and easy over the court, like those tall kids in California who play 365 days a year in a kind of lazy, expert boredom. Robert had a habit of talking jovially and half-irritably to himself when he missed a shot, looking up to heaven and muttering under his breath, "Weaver! *Weaver!* Why don't you just give up? Why don't you just go home?" He had seen his father looking down at him, smiling, and knew that his father understood the mumbled tirade he was delivering to himself. He had grinned and waved his racket and slammed the next three services so hard no returns were possible. . . .

Nelson walked up Madison Avenue toward the office of Marshall and Co., toward the formal and intricate sheets of figures waiting on his desk, toward the neat, professional, bookkeeper's 2 he was proud of. . . .

As he walked he wondered where his son would be sent to meet the enemy. Africa? Australia? India? England? Russia? Desert, plain, mountain, jungle, seacoast—and a twenty-three-year-old boy, ex-swimmer, ex-tennis-player, ex-eater of great sandwiches and drinker of cold beer, ex-lover of his father, hungry and full of jokes and ready for any climate, while his father, full of his slack fifty years, walked daily to his office . . .

Nelson walked along Madison Avenue before the windows of the fine shops. Two women passed him and a high woman's voice said, "Taffeta. Baby-blue taffeta, shirred, with the back bare down to the hips. It has a startling effect."

It never occurred to me it could happen, Nelson thought, walking slowly and blindly away from the station where his son had set off to battle. There was one war and that was all. It's my fault. I had a son, but I didn't take my responsibility seriously enough. I worked and I dressed him and fed him and sent him to a good college and bought him books and gave him money to take out girls and took him with me on vacations to Vermont, but I didn't take my responsibility seriously enough. I worked, and it wasn't easy, and I was poor for a long time and only the poor know how hard it is to stop being poor. I worked, but for the wrong things. I've added millions of rows of figures, detailed the maneuverings of many corporations, year by year, and sometimes it was eighteen hours a day and no time for meals. . . . Nonsense! I'm guilty. I should've been out stopping this. . . . I am nearly the same age as Hitler. He could do something to kill my son. I should've been doing something to save him. I'm guilty. I should be ashamed to stand in the same room with my son in his lieutenant's green blouse. Money . . . I thought about the grocer, the insurance man, the electric light company . . . Nonsense, nonsense . . . I've wasted my life. I'm an old man and alone and my son has gone to war and all I did was pay rent and taxes. I was playing with toys. I was smoking opium. Me and millions like me. The war was being fought for twenty years and I didn't know it. I waited for my son to grow up and fight it for me. I should've been out screaming on street corners, I should've grabbed people by their lapels in trains, in libraries and restaurants and yelled at them. "Love, understand, put down your guns, forget your profit, remember God . . ." I should have walked on foot through Germany and France and England and America. I should've preached on the dusty roads and used a rifle when necessary. I stayed in the one city and paid the grocer. Versailles, Manchuria, Ethiopia, Warsaw, Madrid—battlefields, battlefields—and I thought there was one war and it was over.

He stopped and looked up. He was sweating now and the salt was in his eyes and he had to rub them to see that he was standing in front of the great monument of a building, serene and immutable, in which, in war and peace, Marshall and Co.

conducted its business. His charts and figures were waiting for him, all the clever, legal, evasive, money-saving numbers that a global dealer in valves and turbines could assemble in this bloody and profitable year to turn over in its solemn annual report to the government of the republic. Depreciation . . . $3,100,456.25.

He looked up at the soaring shining building sharp against the soft summer sky.

He stood there, before the graven entrance, and people jostled him and came and went, but he didn't go in.

FAITH AT SEA

Lieutenant Peter Gifford Lawrence stood on the foredeck of the SS *Rascoe*, holding on lightly to the canvas-sheathed three-inch gun as the bow dipped and trembled in the harsh chop of the North Atlantic. Twelve men of the gun crew stood at ease before him, shifting easily with the soaring lift and fall of the SS *Rascoe* as she chewed busily into the slate waves that had been hacking at her for six days, getting stronger and stronger as the 6,000-ton tramp steamer ploughed at nine knots toward England.

"The duties of the gun captain," Constantini was chanting, like a child in school. "A, on manning gun, reports through sight-setter to group control officer when gun is ready. B, operates plug as necessary. C, calls 'Ready,' to pointer when breech is closed . . ."

Lawrence only half listened as Constantini's voice droned on, in the regular Thursday afternoon gunnery class that Lawrence conducted to keep the Navy gun crew alert and interested on the long, monotonous trips. He looked at the twelve men outlined in mufflers and coats, against the low-hanging cold sun. These, plus the four men on duty now at the rear gun, had been given him by the Navy to guard the gray and shabby and valuable life of the SS *Rascoe*, and as always, when he saw them assembled he felt with a mixture of amusement and pity how old he was.

He was only thirty-five, but except for Farrell, the Chief Petty Officer, who was older than he, and Benson, the gunner's mate, who was twenty-five, all the men were twenty-one or under, their faces bronzed and unlined and boyish, always solemn and youthfully important when they were assembled like this for any official function, and especially solemn today because they had lost the convoy the night before in a storm and were now plodding over the gray wastes toward port, vulnerable and alone.

"He is responsible for the conduct, efficiency and spirit of the crew," Constantini was saying, "and must be made to realize that he is the representative of his battery officer."

"Very good," Lawrence said. "Harris."

"Yes, sir." Harris stood stiffly at attention.

"The duties of the sight setter."

"To set the sights," Harris rattled off glibly, "and to transmit all communications between gun and group control officer."

Lawrence looked up over Harris's head to the bridge. Captain Linsey, his beard patchy and crooked in the wind, was peering angrily down at what he called the Navy kindergarten.

"To call 'Set,'" Harris was saying, "to pointer when sights have been set . . ."

Suddenly Harris stopped. Lawrence turned from looking at Linsey on the bridge. The man next to Harris, William Doneger, was on his knees by Harris's side, gripping Harris's arm with a tortured, clutching hand. Harris stood there stupidly, frightened, looking blankly at the sweating tense face.

"Doneger . . ." Lawrence started toward him. Doneger let loose his grip and dropped, bent over and rocking, to the deck.

Constantini sank swiftly to his knees and took Doneger's head in his hands, tenderly.

"What is it?" Lawrence kneeled beside the two of them, with the other men crowded silent and helpless around them.

Doneger looked up at him wildly, the sweat breaking from his forehead, even in this bitter winter evening.

"He's been sick all day, sir," Constantini said, his hands almost unconsciously going slowly and soothingly over his friend's forehead. "Terrible bellyache, sir."

Lawrence looked down at the suffering boy. His lips were bleeding from biting them and his face had grown terribly, greenly pale, morbid and alarming in the cold Atlantic dusk. His legs pulled spasmodically and unreasonably as he lay on the wet deck.

"Let's get him below," Lawrence said. "To my quarters." There was no doctor on board and Lawrence's quarters had the medical chest and served as clinic for the Navy men.

Constantini got Doneger under the armpits and one of the other men got him around the knees and they started down with him. Constantini was a broad, powerful boy and held his friend firmly and lightly and maneuvered him delicately up the steps, his face tense and wary as he attempted to beat the cruel roll of the ship which at any moment threatened to smash the sick boy against a bulkhead.

Lawrence looked out across the ocean for a last survey. The water hissed by the SS *Rascoe* and the gray waves piled endlessly and monotonously on top of each other and the clouds came down, and that was all. He swallowed a little drily, thinking of Doneger lying racked and contorted in his room, then braced his shoulders consciously and walked slowly toward his quarters.

When he opened the door, Doneger was lying on the extra berth and Constantini was whispering to him, a steady, soft stream of comforting words. Constantini had a deep melodious voice, like a singer, and it sounded like a lullaby as he whispered to his friend.

"Nothing at all, William, nothing at all." He was the only one on the ship who called Doneger William. All the other men called him Bill and Billy, but Constantini gave him his full and proper name, like a doting mother, at all times. "Something you ate. I've had bellyaches in my time. . . ." Constantini was seventeen years old. "I thought I was going to split down the middle and two hours later I'd be out eating two plates of spaghetti and a quart of dago red. . . ."

When he saw Lawrence come into the room, he stopped his whispering and stood up at attention, trying to make his face impassive and military. But he had a child's face with deep soft-brown Italian eyes, with heavy curled black eyelashes, and a full, almost girlish mouth, and the military mask at the moment was not deceptive.

Lawrence looked down at the suffering boy. Doneger looked up at him wanly. "Sorry, sir," he whispered.

"Sssh," Lawrence said.

"He's been puking, sir," Constantini said. "All day, sir . . ."

Lawrence sighed and sat down on the berth next to Doneger. That's what it's going to turn out to be, he thought, as he put his hand on the boy's side. The worst possible thing . . .

The right side was swollen and tight and Doneger jumped even with the slightest pressure.

"He has a very sensitive belly, sir," Constantini was speaking quickly and anxiously, as though somehow his words and explanations could make the disease less. "I took him to my cousin's wedding and he got drunk faster than anyone else, even faster than the sixteen-year-old girls . . . We had a stew yesterday that was a little greasy and maybe . . ."

"He has appendicitis, Salvatore," Lawrence said slowly.

Constantini looked at his friend's face in silence. Doneger closed his eyes. Lying down here, in the warm stateroom, on a dry bed, he seemed more comfortable, better able to meet the pain.

"Everything will be all right, William," Constantini murmured to Doneger. "The Lieutenant has already diagnosed the disease."

The door opened and Captain Linsey came in. He stood above Doneger, staring down at him, without a word, his mouth curled, as always when he had anything to do with the Navy men on board his ship, into a sour and ancient snarl.

"Sick," Linsey sad. "This son-of-a-bitch is very sick."

"Yes," Lawrence said. Captain Linsey would make amusing conversation after the war at dinner parties in Boston. Crusty old merchant seadog. Ignored the Navy. Ignored the war, even in the middle of a pack of submarines.

"This son-of-a-bitch'll die." Captain Linsey leaned over and peered harshly into the pale suffering face.

Very amusing after the war at dinner parties, Lawrence thought. Right now I'd like to kill him.

"We'll take care of him," Lawrence said.

Suddenly Captain Linsey poked Doneger in the side with a huge, wrinkled finger. Doneger cried and jumped. "Sorry, Sonny," Captain Linsey said. He turned to Lawrence. "Ready to bust. Boy out with me on the way to Wilhelmshaven in 1931 died in three days. Same thing."

Out of the corner of his eye, Lawrence saw Constantini look quickly down at Doneger, then look up and take a long, deep breath.

"Please," Lawrence said. "I'll come up to the bridge later and you can tell me whatever you . . ."

"This son-of-a-bitch needs an operation."

"There's no doctor on board."

Captain Linsey sucked at the wet ends of his mustache, looked with crazy slyness at Lawrence. "We won't make port for seven days. At least. He ain't going to last no week."

I'd like to kill him, Lawrence thought, looking up at Captain Linsey's old, harsh seaman's face. I'd like to kill him, but he's right, he's right.

"I thought we could freeze it," Lawrence said. "After all, we have ice. Maybe it'll subside . . ."

"Too late." Captain Linsey wagged his head finally. "Surgery. Surgery or nothing."

"There're no surgeons here," Lawrence said loudly. "If you insist on arguing, let's get out of this room."

"You ever see an operation?" Captain Linsey asked.

"Yes." Lawrence's brother-in-law was a fashionable surgeon and over a period of ten years Lawrence had seen seven or eight operations. "That isn't the same thing."

"There was a Dutchman we took to Capetown in 1927," Captain Linsey said. "A doctor. Studied in America. He left a book on board. All kinds of operations. Every once in a while I read in it. Very interesting reading. I bet it's got appendicitis in it."

"That's ridiculous," Lawrence stood up and went over to the door. "Thank you for your interest, Captain . . ."

Captain Linsey touched Doneger's head. "Fever. I bet it's over 104. An operation really isn't so much. A little common sense and a little nerve. What the hell, what has this boy got to lose?" He leaned close to Doneger and spoke with surprising softness. "Sonny, you got any objections to being operated on?"

Doneger stared at Constantini. Constantini turned away, giving no answer one way or another with his eyes.

"I have no objections," Doneger said faintly.

Captain Linsey strode briskly toward the door. "I'll send the book down," he said cheerfully. "We'll save the son-of-a-bitch yet." He clapped Lawrence on the back. "I'd do it myself only I'm old and jumpy and I've drunk too much whisky in my day. I'll be on the bridge. I'll keep this tub as steady as possible."

He went out quickly.

Lawrence closed his eyes so that he wouldn't have to look at Doneger or Crowley or Constantini, all standing stiffly watching him.

A moment later a seaman came in with a worn and broken-backed book. He put it on the table and went out. Crowley and Doneger and Constantini and Lawrence all looked at the fat, dog-eared book, lying alone on the table. Lawrence stood up and went over and opened to the index. Under A Pg. 941—Appendectomy.

The first time he read through it, the words were a weird and incomprehensible blur. He looked up once or twice only to see the staring, serious eyes of the three other men scanning his face, as though they somehow could tell from that distance whether or not the words he was reading were of any value to him or not.

Lawrence took off his coat and started slowly to read it from the beginning, once more.

Before operating, try to locate the situation of the appendix. The incision should be over the seat of the disease. In the rare left-sided cases and in median cases, the incision is median . . .

The words began to group themselves in his mind into English sentences, capable of being understood by a man who could read and write.

In an acute case in a man I separate the muscular fibres. Battle's incision at the outer edge of the rectus muscle is preferred by many surgeons . . .

In a biology course in college he had dissected the earthworm, the frog, the white rat—but all dead, beyond the reach of pain, unmoved by clumsiness or error.

If there be infection, surround the region involved with packs of plain gauze, each strip being two and a half inches wide, fifteen inches long, and four layers in thickness. Pass a ligature through the meso appendix as shown in Fig. 691, A, tie the ligature and . . .

Fig. 691, A, was very simple and if flesh and muscle and organ were anything like the diagram, it was conceivable that a deft, though unpracticed man might be able to manage . . .

"William," Lawrence said. "Are you sure?"

Doneger sighed. "I'm sure."

"Crowley," Lawrence said. "Go to the galley and get a pot of boiling water."

"Yes, sir," Crowley said, and went out softly, already making a hospital out of the room.

Lawrence went back to the close print of the book. He read and re-read, studied the diagrams until he felt he could draw them with his eyes closed.

He stood up and unlocked the medical chest. He threw open the doors and stared at the rows of bottles, the serried bandages, the fateful gleaming instruments. Behind him he heard the soft child's voice of Constantini, rough with the accent of the streets of New York, soft with compassion and fear.

"It ain't hardly nothing, William. A cousin of mine had this and he was operated on and three days later he slept with the nurse." Constantini had a cousin for all eventualities of discussion, naval and civilian. "Everybody ought to have his appendix out. They don't do you no good. None at all. If I had the time I'd have 'em out myself. . . ."

Lawrence stared at the bottles, the bandages, the steel instruments. He made his eyes go slowly and calmly from one thing to another in the chest, taking a deliberate inventory. The thing is, he thought, not to hurry. After all, men have done more difficult things than this. The instruments are there, the one can of ether, the bandage, the scalpel, the needles, the catgut, the clamps, the sponges, the alcohol, sulfanilamide. And the Navy had given him a course in First Aid. How to stop bleeding. How to avoid gangrene. How to set a broken leg.

"You hardly feel it," Constantini was saying in his deep melodious boy's voice. "You take a little nap. You wake up. Appendix absent. You feel a little stiff for a day or two, you get a good rest, the other guys stand your watches, you read the magazines and drink hot soup. You get to England, you get three weeks sick leave, you'll have the time of your life. The English girls're crazy about American sailors. I got a cousin in the merchant marine and he says that an American in London is like a king, far as the girls're concerned. They can't do enough for them . . ."

Why, Lawrence thought with a remote and bitter detachment, did this have to happen the first time we lost a convoy? In a convoy the boy could be transferred to one of the cruisers accompanying them and there a first-rate naval surgeon in a shining, brilliantly equipped operating room would do the job as a matter of simple routine in ten minutes.

Crowley came in with the pot of hot water and Lawrence put the scalpel, the needles and the clamps into it.

"Anything I can do," Constantini said, as Lawrence watched the steel gleaming dully as it sank among the bubbles of the boiling water. "Anything at all."

Lawrence nodded. "There'll be plenty for you to do. Clear that table and get a sheet out of the locker and spread it over it." Constantini listened eagerly and nodded. "Wash your hands first."

While Crowley and Constantini scrubbed their hands and the strong smell of the soap pricked his nostrils, Lawrence re-read, slowly, the entire description of the operation.

Even after he had finished and after the gentle watery sound of scrubbing behind him had long ceased, he sat with his head in his hands, staring at the page before him.

He stood up. Well, that was that . . .

He turned briskly and without words he and Constantini and Crowley lifted Doneger onto the white-covered table. He washed and scrubbed his hands with alcohol. Gently, he shaved the slight downy fuzz from the boy's belly. Then he washed it with alcohol.

Crowley behaved wonderfully. He was a little, impassive Irishman, to whom all things seemed to come as a matter of course, promotions, overwork, murders, drownings, wars. Lawrence was glad it was Crowley who had silently volunteered for this job.

Constantini, too, handled Doneger with soft hands, lifting him gently and securely, making no unnecessary move. Together they bound Doneger to the table with linen bandage, so that the roll of the ship would not throw him off the table.

Lawrence noticed that the ship had swung around and was heading directly into the wind and was much steadier now. He would remember to thank Captain Linsey later.

He took the ether cone and stood at Doneger's shoulder. Doneger and Constantini and seven or eight of the other boys had had their heads shaven when they were last in the States. They had done it as a kind of joke, after Lawrence had complained at inspection that they were letting their hair grow too long. All seven of them had marched solemnly back onto the SS *Rascoe* from their shore leaves and had with one gesture swept their hats off their heads as they reported in. Lawrence had stared at the seven shining pates, scarred with the incredibly numerous battles of childhood, and had lowered his eyes to keep from laughing and had said, "Very good."

They had saluted and swept out and he had heard them roaring with laughter on the deck . . .

Doneger's head, now with a slight baby fuzz standing up all over it, lay flatly, in the shadows, on the table in the small cabin as the old plates on the SS *Rascoe* creaked and wailed under the attack of the sea. . . .

"All right, William," Lawrence said softly. "Are you ready now?"

"I'm ready, sir." Doneger spoke in a whisper and smiled up at him.

Lawrence put the cone gently over the boy's face and said, "Breathe deeply." He poured the ether in and the smell, sweet and deadly leaked into the cabin, making it strange and deathly suddenly. "Count," Lawrence said. "Keep counting."

"One, two, three," Doneger said clearly. "Four, five, six, seven, eight . . ." The young voice began to blur and thicken. "Nine, ten, eleven, twelve, thir—thir . . ." The voice mumbled heavily and wearily through the cone. The long chubby body on the table relaxed for the first time and Crowley gently straightened the legs out. The voice died away completely and the noise of the creaking plates of the old ship was the only sound to be heard.

Lawrence lifted the ether cone. Doneger's face was calm and showed no trace of pain. He gave the cone to Constantini. "If I tell you to," he said, "put this over his face. In case he moves . . ."

"Yes, sir," Constantini said, and moved quickly to Doneger's head.

Lawrence went to the pot of boiling water, and with a forceps took out the instruments he had put in there to sterilize. Crowley had arranged a clean towel on the bunk and Lawrence put the instruments there in a neat and shining row, remembering how dentists who had filled his teeth had done the same thing.

He picked up the scalpel and arranged the lamp so that its full glare fell on the bare stomach of the sleeping boy.

The skin was very pink, and there was a firm small layer of fat under it. Doneger was very young and his belly still had a round little baby-swell. He was breathing softly and the muscles trembled rhythmically and gently in the harsh light of the single lamp.

How smooth, how subtle, how complex, Lawrence thought, how close to death. How vulnerable to knife and powder. How irrevocably naked to damage. He closed his eyes for a moment, unable to look any more at the smooth childish skin. With his eyes closed and the moaning and creaking of the tumbling ship in his ears, it all seemed dreamlike and impossible. He, Peter Gifford Lawrence, gently reared, nursed and fed and tended all his years by mother and aunt and teacher and doctor, every boyhood scratch mercurochromed and overbandaged, soft-blanketed sleeper in neat, well-ventilated rooms, student at Harvard where he had taken notes on Plato and Geoffrey Chaucer, on the architecture of the Renaissance and the metrics of John Milton, Peter Gifford Lawrence, gentleman, formal guest at pleasant dinners, polite talker to old ladies at Lenox garden parties, dealer in books and fine prints, now standing scalpel in hand in the cramped, peeling First-Officer's quarters of a wheezing freighter groaning and heaving in a Middle Atlantic gale, with four miles of black sea water and countless drowned sailors under the keel, the prey of deadly vessels that struck unseen and mortal in the turn of a man's head . . .

Battle's incision at the outer edge of the rectus muscle is preferred by many surgeons . . . After opening the peritoneum examine very gently to detect the situation of the . . . This divides the mucous membrane, submucous tissue and muscular coat . . .

He opened his eyes and looked up. Constantini was staring at him. In the soft girlish eyes, beside the worry for his friend's agony, there was deep trust, deep confidence that this kindly, efficient, understanding, courageous man, this officer who had been designated by great authority to guide his wartime fate, would, this time and all times, do well what had to be done. There was no doubt in the soft steady eyes of Salvatore Constantini.

Lawrence bent his head and firmly made the necessary incision . . .

When the operation was over and Doneger had been gently lifted into the extra bunk and Constantini had silently taken the watch at his side, Lawrence opened the door and stepped out onto the deck. The black wind flung bitter spray into his face and he had to half-shut his eyes against it. But he stood there, holding onto the rail, peering sightlessly into the roaring darkness, hardly thinking, hardly feeling, rolling crazily and aimlessly with the roll of the ship.

He stood there drunkenly for a long time, then suddenly turned and went into his room. Doneger was lying there, steady and still, the ether still in control. Constantini sat quietly at his side, never taking his eyes off the pale, exhausted face.

Lawrence lay down in all his clothes and slept immediately.

When he awoke, he opened his eyes slowly and came up deeply from the well of sleep, as though he had slept for weeks on end. Slowly he became aware of Constantini sitting across the room from him, still looking steadfastly at Doneger, as though he hadn't moved all night.

Lawrence opened his eyes wide.

"Good morning, Lieutenant." Constantini smiled shyly at him. His eyes were sunken and he rubbed them like a sleepy infant.

"Morning, Salvatore." Lawrence sat up suddenly and looked at Doneger, remembering in a rush that across from him lay a man whom he had operated upon the night before. Doneger was awake, and drowsily smiled, his face creased by a kind of remote pain.

"Hello, Lieutenant," Doneger whispered.

Lawrence jumped out of his bunk. "How are you?"

"Fine," Doneger whispered. "First class. Thanks."

Lawrence peered at him closely. There were wrinkles of pain in the boy's smooth face, but there was a little color in the cheeks and something in the eyes that seemed to announce that death had once and for all passed by.

Lawrence looked at Constantini. "You get any sleep last night?"

"Not much, sir. I'm pleased to watch William."

"Get below and get some sleep. Someone else'll watch William."

"Yes, sir." Constantini looked shyly at him and then turned to Doneger. "My God," he whispered, as Lawrence poured some water to wash, "will you have a picnic with those English girls . . ."

And he touched his friend's forehead lightly and chuckled as he went out and deep, deep, from the depths of his eighteen years and recovery from death, Doneger chuckled softly in return.

Later in the day, Lawrence started forward toward the bow gun, where the men were assembled for the interrupted examination in gunnery. The sun was shining and the ocean was a sharp, wintry blue, with the whitecaps in the distance looking like the bobbing sails of a regatta with a million entries. He had left Doneger smiling and sipping tea and the bright wind felt festive and alive against his freshly shaven face. He saw the cluster of blue uniforms and the ruddy faces of the gun crew around the gun and heard Constantini's voice, melodious and terribly earnest, chanting in final review before his arrival. Lawrence smiled to himself and was proud of the Navy and the red-faced earnest boys, and the gun and the

SS *Rascoe* and himself, abroad, dependable and unafraid, on the wide ocean.

" 'Tention!" Benson called as he approached, and the boys stiffened rigidly, their faces stern and set, their hands tight at their sides. Lawrence looked sternly at them, carrying out his share of the military drama.

He looked at them and felt once more with the old amusement and pity how old he was at the age of thirty-five, confronted by and responsible for these large, determined, valuable, fearless children.

"At ease," he said.

The tight little knot relaxed and the men shuffled about, making themselves comfortable. They kept their eyes on Lawrence, seriously. Constantini's lips mumbled inaudibly as he ran over the list of questions he might be asked to answer.

"We'll go right into it," Lawrence said. "Harris . . ." he started with the boy nearest him. "What're the duties of the first loader?"

"To receive the shell from the second loader," Harris said. "And to load the gun."

"Levine." Lawrence spoke to the next man. "Duties of the second loader?"

"To pass shells to the first loader." Levine said carefully. "To arrange shells on deck in rear of gun in probable arc of train."

"Constantini . . ." Lawrence went down the line. He saw Constantini's face tense almost painfully with anticipation. "What are the duties of the third loader?"

Constantini's lips started to move. Then he licked them uneasily. He took in a deep breath, looked suddenly, blankly and despairingly at Lawrence. Lawrence glanced at him and saw that all knowledge had fled from his head, like an actor on opening night, with four weeks of rehearsals behind him, who is stricken dumb by the overpowering desire to do well.

A deep red flush surged up over Constantini's collar and stained his cheeks, his ears. He licked his lips in misery, looked straight ahead, hopelessly . . .

Lawrence looked away, called the next man, Moran, went on with the questioning.

Moran answered the question briskly.

One by one, Lawrence went down the line of men. Each man snapped out his answer, their voices ringing clear and triumphant in the bright wind. Once more it was Constantini's turn.

Lawrence looked surreptitiously at him. He was next in line and he was standing as stiff as though all the admirals of all the fleets of the world were passing him in review. His jaws were clenched and the muscles stood out in them like rope. His eyes stared ahead of him like a man watching the execution of his father, wild, hopeless, full of guilt.

Lawrence knew in his heart that no matter what question he put to Constantini, no answer would come from that mourning brain, no word pass those locked, despairing lips. For a moment Lawrence thought of passing him up and going on to the next man. But then, to the shame of Constantini's ignorance and defection would be added the ignominy of official pity.

"Constantini," Lawrence said as crisply as he could, hoping to shock him out of his trancelike trauma. He carefully sought out the simplest, most transparent, easily answered question in the whole book. "Constantini," he said, slowly and clearly and loudly, "what is the purpose of shrapnel?"

Constantini did not move. The tongue froze between the lips, the eyes stared without hope across the Atlantic Ocean, while no answer came to show this good man, this Boston Lieutenant who had done a brave and noble thing to save his friend's life that he, Salvatore Constantini, loved and admired him and would be grateful to him for the rest of his life. The blush settled like a permanent blight on his cheeks, but no answer came from the rockbound brain. The deep, ordinary thanks that a man could give by the crisp performance of his duty could not be given. William lived and Salvatore failed the man who had saved him.

Suddenly the tears started from his eyes and rolled down his rigid cheeks.

Lawrence looked at the weeping boy, staring blindly out to sea, among the men who kindly stared out to sea with him. Lawrence saw the bitter tears and almost put out his hand to comfort the boy, but held back just in time, since comfort now, before his ten friends, would be agony later.

Lawrence glanced once more at him and tried to call the next man's name and ask him the purpose of shrapnel, but the name stuck in his throat and he turned his back on the men and wept and felt the tears cold on his cheeks without surprise.

GUNNERS' PASSAGE

"In Brazil," Whitejack was saying, "the problem was girls. American girls."

They were lying on the comfortable cots with the mosquito netting looped gracefully over their heads and the barracks quiet and empty except for the two of them and shaded and cool when you remembered that outside the full sun of Africa stared down.

"Three months in the jungle, on rice and monkey meat." Whitejack lit a large, long, nickel cigar and puffed deeply, squinting up at the tin roof. "When we got to Rio, we felt we deserved an American girl. So the Lieutenant and Johnny and myself, we got the telephone directory of the American Embassy, and we went down the list, calling up likely names—secretaries, typists, interpreters, filing clerks. . . ." Whitejack grinned up at the ceiling. He had a large, sunburned, rough face, that was broken into good-looks by the white teeth of his smile, and his speech was Southern, but not the kind of Southern that puts a Northerner's teeth on edge.

"It was the Lieutenant's idea, and by the time we got to the Q's he was ready to give up but we hit paydirt on the S's." Slowly he blew out a long draught of cigar smoke. "Uh-uh," he said, closing his eyes reflectively. "Two months and eleven days of honey and molasses. Three tender and affectionate American girls as loving as the day is long, with their own flat. Beer in the icebox from Sunday to Sunday, steaks big enough to saddle a mule with, and nothing to do, just lie on the beach in the afternoon and go swimmin' when the mood seized yuh. On per diem."

"How were the girls?" Stais asked. "Pretty?"

"Well, Sergeant," Whitejack paused and pursed his lips with thoughtful honesty. "To tell you the truth, Sergeant, the girls the Lieutenant and Johnny Moffat had were as smart and pretty as chipmunks. Mine . . ." Once more he paused. "Ordinarily, my girl would find herself hard put to collect a man in the middle of a full division of infantry soldiers. She was small and runty and she had less curves than a rifle barrel, and she wore glasses. But from the first time she looked at me, I could see she wasn't interested in Johnny or the Lieutenant. She looked at me and behind her glasses her eyes were soft and hopeful and humble and appealing." Whitejack flicked the cigar ash off into the little tin can on his bare chest he was using as an ash tray. "Sometimes," he said slowly, "a man feels mighty small if he just thinks of himself and turns down an appeal like that. Let me tell you something, Sergeant, I was in Rio two months and eleven days and I didn't look at another woman. All those dark-brown women walkin' along the beach three-quarters out of their bathing suits, just wavin' it in front of your face. . . . I didn't look at them. This runty, skinny little thing with glasses was the most lovin' and satisfactory and decent little person a man could possibly conceive of, and a man'd just have to be hog-greedy with sex to have winked an eye at another woman." Whitejack doused his cigar, took his ash tray off his chest, rolled over on his belly, adjusted the towel properly over his bare buttocks. "Now," he said, "I'm going to get myself a little sleep. . . ."

In a moment Whitejack was snoring gently, his tough mountaineer's face tucked childishly into the crook of his arm. Outside the barracks the native boy hummed low and wild to himself as he ironed a pair of suntan trousers on the shady side of the building. From the field, two hundred yards away, again and again came the sliding roar of engines climbing or descending the afternoon sky.

Stais closed his eyes wearily. Ever since he'd got into Accra he had done nothing but sleep and lie on his cot, day-dreaming, listening to Whitejack talk.

"Hi," Whitejack had said, as Stais had come slowly into the barracks two days before, "which way you going?"

"Home," Stais had said, smiling wearily as he did every time he said it. "Going home. Which way you going?"

"Not home." Whitejack had grinned a little. "Not home at all."

Stais liked to listen to Whitejack. Whitejack talked about America, about the woods of the Blue Ridge Mountains where he had been in the forestry service, about his mother's cooking and how he had owned great dogs who had been extraordinary at finding a trail and holding it, about how they had tried hunting deer in the hills from the medium bomber, no good because of the swirling winds rising from the gorges, about pleasant indiscriminate week-end parties in the woods with his friend Johnny Moffat and the girls from the mill in the next town. . . . Stais had been away from America for nineteen months now and Whitejack's talk made his native country seem present and pleasantly real to him.

"There was a man in my town by the name of Thomas Wolfe," Whitejack had said irrelevantly that morning. "He was a great big feller and he went away to New York to be an author. Maybe you heard of him?"

"Yes," said Stais. "I read two books of his."

"Well, I read that book of his," said Whitejack, "and the people in town were yellin' to lynch him for awhile, but I read that book and he got that town down fair and proper, and when they brought him back dead I came down from the hills and I went to his funeral. There were a lot of important people from New York and over to Chapel Hill down for the funeral and it was a hot day, too, and I'd never met the feller, but I felt it was only right to go to his funeral after readin' his book. And the whole town was there, very quiet, although just five years before they were yellin' to lynch him, and it was a sad and impressive sight and I'm glad I went."

And another time, the slow deep voice rolling between sleep and dreams in the shaded heat. . . . "My mother takes a quail and bones it, then she scoops out a great big sweet potato and lays some bacon on it, then she puts the quail in and cooks it slow for three hours, bastin' it with butter all the time. . . . You got to try that some time. . . ."

"Yes," said Stais, "I will."

Stais did not have a high priority number and there seemed to be a flood of colonels surging toward America, taking all the seats on the C-54's setting out westward, so he'd had to wait. It hadn't been bad. Just to lie down, stretched full-out, unbothered, these days, was holiday enough after Greece, and anyway he didn't want to arrive home, in front of his mother, until he'd stopped looking like a tired old man. And the barracks had been empty and quiet and the chow good at the transient mess and you could get Coca-Cola and chocolate milk at the PX. The rest of the enlisted men in Whitejack's crew were young and ambitious and were out swimming all day and going to the movies or playing poker in another barracks all night, and Whitejack's talk was smooth and amusing in the periods between sleep and dreams. Whitejack was an aerial photographer and gunner in a mapping-and-survey squadron and he'd been in Alaska and Brazil and back to the States and now was on his way to India, full of conversation. He was in a Mitchell squadron and the whole squadron was supposed to be on its way together, but two of the Mitchells had crashed and burned on the take-off at Natal, as Whitejack's plane had circled the field, waiting to form up. The rest of the squadron had been held at Natal and Whitejack's plane had been sent on to Accra across the ocean, by itself.

Vaguely and slowly, lying on the warm cot, with the wild song of the Negro boy outside the window, Stais thought of the two Mitchells burning between sea and jungle three thousand miles away, and other planes burning elsewhere, and what it was going to be like sitting down in the armchair in his own house and looking across the room at his mother, and the pretty Viennese girl in Jerusalem, and the DC3 coming down slowly, like an angel in the dusk to the rough secret pasture in the Peloponnesian hills. . . .

He fell asleep. His bones knit gently into dreams on the soft cot, with the sheets, in the quiet barracks, and he was over Athens again, with the ruins pale and shining on the hills, and the fighters boring in, and Lathrop saying, over the intercom, as they persisted in to a hundred, fifty yards, twisting, swiftly and shiftily in the bright Greek sky, "They grounded all the students today. They have the instructors up this afternoon . . ." And, suddenly, and wildly, fifty feet over Ploesti, with Liberators going down into the filth in dozens, flaming. . . . Then swimming off the white beach at Bengasi with the dead boys playing in the mild, tideless swell, then the parachute pulling at every muscle in his body, then the green and forest blue of Minnesota woods and his father, fat and small, sleeping on pine needles on his Sunday off, then Athens again, Athens . . .

"I don't know what's come over the Lieutenant," a new voice was saying as Stais came out of his dream. "He passes us on the field and he just don't seem to see us."

Stais opened his eyes. Novak, a farm boy from Oklahoma, was sitting on the edge of Whitejack's bed, talking. "It has all the guys real worried." He had a high, shy, rather girlish voice. "I used to think they never came better than the Lieutenant . . . Now . . ." Novak shrugged. "If he does see you, he snaps at you like he was General George Patton."

"Maybe," Whitejack said, "maybe seeing Lieutenant Brogan go down in Natal . . . He and Brogan were friends since they were ten years old. Like as if I saw Johnny Moffat go down . . ."

"It's not that." Novak went over to his own cot and got out his writing pad. "It began back in Miami four weeks ago. Didn't you notice it?"

"I noticed it," Whitejack said slowly.

"You ought to ask him about it." Novak started writing a letter. "You and him are good friends. After all, going into combat now, it's bad, the Lieutenant just lookin' through us when he passes us on the field. You don't think he's drunk all the time, do you?"

"He's not drunk."

"You ought to ask him."

"Maybe I will." Whitejack sat up, tying the towel around his lean middle. "Maybe I will." He looked forlornly down at his stomach. "Since I got into the Army, I've turned pig-fat. On the day I took the oath, I was twenty-eight and one-half inches around the waist. Today I'm thirty-two and three-quarters, if

I'm an inch. The Army . . . Maybe I shouldn't've joined. I was in a reserved profession, and I was the sole support of an ailing mother."

"Why did you join?" Stais asked.

"Oh," Whitejack smiled at him, "you're awake. Feeling any better, Sergeant?"

"Feeling fine, thanks. Why did you join?"

"Well . . ." Whitejack rubbed the side of his jaw. "Well . . . I waited and I waited. I sat up in my cabin in the hills and I tried to avoid listenin' to the radio, and I waited and I waited, and finally I went downtown to my mother and I said, 'Ma'am, I just can't wait any longer,' and I joined up."

"When was that?" Stais asked.

"Eight days . . ." Whitejack lay down again, plumping the pillow under his head. "Eight days after Pearl Harbor."

"Sergeant," Novak said, "Sergeant Stais, you don't mind if I tell my girl you're a Greek, do you?"

"No," Stais said gravely. "I don't mind. You know, I was born in Minnesota."

"I know," said Novak, writing industriously. "But your parents came from Greece. My girl'll be very interested, your parents coming from Greece and you bombing Greece and being shot down there."

"What do you mean, your girl?" Whitejack asked. "I thought you said she was going around with a Technical Sergeant in Flushing, Long Island."

"That's true," Novak said apologetically. "But I still like to think of her as my girl."

"It's the ones that stay at home," said Whitejack darkly, "that get all the stripes and all the girls. My motto is: Don't write to a girl once you get out of pillow-case distance from her."

"I like to write to this girl in Flushing, Long Island," Novak said, his voice shy but stubborn. Then to Stais, "How many days were you in the hills before the Greek farmers found you?"

"Fourteen," said Stais.

"And how many of you were wounded?"

"Three. Out of seven. The others were dead."

"Maybe," Whitejack said, "he doesn't like to talk about it, Charley."

"Oh, I'm sorry." Novak looked up, his young, unlined face crossed with concern.

"That's all right," Stais said. "I don't mind."

"Did you tell them you were a Greek, too?" Novak asked.

"When one finally showed up who could speak English."

"That must be funny," Novak said reflectively. "Being a Greek, bombing Greece, not speaking the language . . . Can I tell my girl they had a radio and they radioed to Cairo . . . ?"

"It's the girl of a Technical Sergeant in Flushing, Long Island," Whitejack chanted. "Why don't you look facts in the face?"

"I prefer it this way," Novak said with dignity.

"I guess you can tell about the radio," Stais said. "It was pretty long ago. Three days later, the DC3 came down through a break in the clouds. It'd been raining all the time and it just stopped for about thirty minutes at dusk and that plane came down throwin' water fifteen feet in the air. . . . We cheered, but we couldn't get up from where we were sitting, any of us, because we were too weak to stand."

"I got to write that to my girl," Novak said. "Too weak to stand."

"Then it started to rain again and the field was hip-deep in mud and when we all got into the DC3, we couldn't get it started," Stais spoke calmly and thoughtfully, as though he were alone, reciting to himself. "We were just bogged down in that Greek mud. Then the pilot got out—he was a captain—and he looked around, with the rain coming down and all those farmers just standing there, sympathizing with him, and nothing anyone could do and he just cursed for ten minutes. He was from San Francisco and he really knew how to curse. Then everybody started breaking branches off the trees in the woods around that pasture, even two of us who couldn't stand one hour before, and we just covered that big DC3 complete with branches and waited for the rain to stop. We just sat in the woods and prayed no German patrols would come out in weather like that. In those three days I learned five words of Greek."

"What are they?" Novak asked.

"*Vouno,*" Stais said, "That means mountain. *Vrohi:* Rains. *Theos:* God. *Avrion:* Tomorrow. And *Yassov:* That means farewell."

"*Yassov,*" Novak said. "Farewell."

"Then the sun came out and the field started to steam and nobody said anything. We just sat there, watching the water dry off the grass, then the puddles started to go here and there, then the mud to cake a little. Then we got into the DC3 and the Greeks pushed and hauled for awhile and we broke loose and got out. And those farmers just standing below waving at us, as though they were seeing us off at Grand Central Station. Ten miles farther on we went right over a German camp. They fired at us a couple of times, but they didn't come anywhere close. The best moment of my whole life was getting into that hospital bed in Cairo, Egypt. I just stood there and looked at it for a whole minute, looking at the sheets. Then I got in very slow."

"Did you ever find out what happened to those Greeks?" Novak asked.

"No," said Stais. "I guess they're still there, waiting for us to come back some day."

There was silence, broken only by the slow scratching of Novak's pen. Stais thought of the thin, dark mountain faces of the men he had last seen, fading away, waving, standing in the scrub and short silver grass of the hill pasture near the Aegean Sea. They had been cheerful and anxious to please, and there was a look on the faces that made you feel they expected to die.

"How many missions were you on?" Novak asked.

"Twenty-one and a half," Stais said. He smiled. "I count the last one as half."

"How old are you?" Novak was obviously keeping the Technical Sergeant's girl carefully posted on all points of interest.

"Nineteen."

"You look older," said Whitejack.

"Yes," said Stais.

"A lot older."

"Yes."

"Did you shoot down any planes?" Novak peered at him shyly, his red face uncertain and embarrassed, like a little boy asking a doubtful question about girls. "Personally?"

"Two," Stais said. "Personally."

"What did you feel?"

"Why don't you leave him alone?" Whitejack said. "He's too tired to keep his eyes open, as it is."

"I felt—relieved," Stais said. He tried to think of what he'd really felt when the tracers went in and the Focke-Wolfe started to smoke like a crazy smudge pot and the German pilot fought wildly for half a second with the cowling and then didn't fight wildly any more. There was no way of telling these men, no way of remembering, in words, himself. "You'll find out," he said. "Soon enough. The sky's full of Germans."

"Japs," Whitejack said. "We're going to India."

"The sky's full of Japs."

There was silence once more, with the echo of the word "Japs" rustling thinly in the long, quiet room, over the empty rows of cots. Stais felt the old waving dizziness starting behind his eyes that the doctor in Cairo had said came from shock or starvation or exposure or all of these things, and lay back, still keeping his eyes open, as it became worse and waved more violently when he closed his eyes.

"One more question," Novak said. "Are—are guys afraid?"

"You'll be afraid," Stais said.

"Do you want to send that back to your girl in Flushing?" Whitejack asked sardonically.

"No," said Novak quietly. "I wanted that for myself."

"If you want to sleep," said Whitejack, "I'll shut this farmer up."

"Oh, no," said Stais, "I'm pleased to talk."

"If you're not careful," Whitejack said, "he'll talk about his girl in Flushing."

"I'd be pleased to hear it," said Stais.

"It's only natural I should want to talk about her," Novak said defensively. "She was the best girl I ever knew in my whole life. I'd've married her if I could."

"My motto," said Whitejack, "is never marry a girl who goes to bed with you the first time out. The chances are she isn't pure. The second time—that, of course, is different." He winked at Stais.

"I was in Flushing, Long Island, taking a five-weeks course in aerial cameras," Novak said, "and I was living at the YMCA. . . ."

"This is where I leave." Whitejack got off the bed and put on his pants.

"The YMCA was very nice. There were bathrooms for every two rooms, and the food was very good," said Novak, talking earnestly to Stais, "but I must confess, I was lonely in Flushing, Long Island. . . ."

"I will be back," Whitejack was buttoning up his shirt, "for the ninth installment."

"As long as you're going out," Novak said to him, "I wish you'd talk to the Lieutenant. It really makes me feel queer passing him, and him just looking through me like I was a window pane."

"Maybe I'll talk to the Lieutenant. And leave the Sergeant alone. Remember he's a tired man who's been to the war and he needs his rest." Whitejack went out.

Novak stared after him. "There's something wrong with him, too," he said. "Just lying on his back here for ten days, reading and sleeping. He never did that before. He was the liveliest man in the United States Air Force. Seeing those two planes go down . . . It's a funny thing, you fly with fellers all over the world, over America, Brazil, Alaska, you watch them shoot porpoises and sharks in gunnery practice over the Gulf Stream, you get drunk with them, go to their weddings, talk to them over the radio with their planes maybe a hundred feet away, in the air—and after all that flying, in one minute, for no reason, two planes go down. Fourteen fellers you've been livin' with for over a year. . . ." Novak shook his head. "There was a particular friend of Whitejack's in one of those planes. Frank Sloan. Just before we left Miami, they had a big fight. Frank went off and married a girl that Whitejack'd been going with off and on for a year, every time we hit Miami. Whitejack told him he was crazy, half the squadron had slept with the lady, and that was true, too, and just to teach him a lesson he'd sleep with her himself after they'd been married. And he did, too. . . ." Novak sighed. "A lot of funny things happen in the army, when fellers've been together a long time and get to know each other real well. And then, one minute, the Mitchell goes down. I guess Whitejack must've felt sort of queer, watching Frankie burn." Novak had put his writing pad down and now he screwed the top on his fountain pen. "The truth is," he said, "I don't feel so solid myself. That's why I like to talk. Especially to you . . . You've been through it. You're young, but you've been through it. But if it's any bother to you, I'll keep quiet. . . ."

"No," said Stais, still lying back, abstractedly wondering whether the waving would get worse or better, "not at all."

"This girl in Flushing, Long Island," Novak said slowly. "It's easy for Whitejack to make fun of me. The girls fall all over themselves chasing after him, he has no real conception of what it's like to be a man like me. Not very good-looking. Not much money. Not an officer. Not humorous. Shy."

Stais couldn't help grinning. "You're going to have a tough time in India."

"I know," Novak said. "I have resigned myself to not having a girl until the armistice. How did you do with the girls in the Middle East?" he asked politely.

"There was a nice Viennese girl in Jerusalem," Stais said

dreamily. "But otherwise zero. You have to be very good unless you're an officer in the Middle East."

"That's what I heard," Novak said sorrowfully. "Well, it won't be so different to me from Oklahoma. That was the nice thing about this girl in Flushing, Long Island. She saw me come into the jewelry store where she worked and . . . I was in my fatigues and I was with a very smooth feller who made a date with her for that night. But she smiled at me, and I knew if I had the guts I could ask her for a date, too. But of course I didn't. But then later that night I was sitting in my room in the YMCA and my phone rang. It was this girl. The other feller had stood her up, she said, and would I take her out." Novak smiled dimly, thinking of that tremulous moment of glory in the small hotel room far away. "I got my fatigues off in one minute and shaved and showered and I picked her up. We went to Coney Island. It was the first time in my entire life I had ever seen Coney Island. It took three and a half weeks for me to finish my course and I went out with that girl every single night. Nothing like that ever happened to me before in my life—a girl who just wanted to see me every night of the week. Then the night before I was due to leave to join my squadron she told me she had got permission to take the afternoon off and she would like to see me off if I let her. I called at the jewelry shop at noon and her boss shook my hand and she had a package under her arm and we got into the subway and we rode to New York City. Then we went into a cafeteria and had a wonderful lunch and she saw me off and gave me the package. It was Schrafft's candy, and she was crying at the gate there, crying for me, and she said she would like me to write, no matter what . . ." Novak paused and Stais could tell that the scene at the gate, the hurrying crowds, the package of Schrafft's chocolates, the weeping young girl, were as clear as the afternoon sunlight to Novak there on the coast of Africa. "So I keep writing," Novak said. "She's written me she has a Technical Sergeant now, but I keep writing. I haven't seen her in a year and a half and what's a girl to do? Do you blame her?"

"No," said Stais, "I don't blame her."

"I hope I haven't bored you," Novak said.

"Not at all." Stais smiled at him. Suddenly the dizziness had gone and he could close his eyes. As he drifted down into that weird and ever-present pool of sleep in which he half-lived these days, he heard Novak say, "Now I have to write my mother."

Outside, the Negro boy sang and the planes grumbled down from the Atlantic and laboriously set out across the Sahara Desert.

Dreams again. Arabs, bundled in rags, driving camels along the perimeter of the field, outlined against the parked Liberators and waiting bombs, two Mitchells still burning on the shores of Brazil and Frank Sloan burning there and circling above him, Whitejack, who had told him he'd sleep with his wife and had, the hills around Jerusalem, gnarled, rocky, dusty, with the powdered green of olive groves set on slopes here and there, clinging against the desert wind, Mitchells slamming along the gorges of the Blue Ridge Mountains, bucking in the updraughts, their guns going, hunting deer, the Mediterranean, bluer than anything in America, below them on the way home from Italy, coming down below oxygen level, with the boys singing dirty songs over the intercom and leave in Alexandria ahead of them. The girl from Flushing, Long Island, quietly going hand in hand with Novak to Coney Island on a summer's night. . . .

It was Whitejack who awakened him. He woke slowly. It

was dark outside and the electric light was shining in his eyes and Whitejack was standing over him, shaking him gently.

"I thought you'd like to know," Whitejack was saying, "your name's on the bulletin board. You're leaving tonight."

"Thanks," Stais said, dimly grateful at being shaken out of the broken and somehow sorrowful dreams.

"I took the liberty of initialing it for you, opposite your name," Whitejack said. "Save you a trip up to the field."

"Thanks," said Stais. "Very kind of you."

"Also," said Whitejack, "There's fried chicken for chow."

Stais pondered over the fried chicken. He was a little hungry, but the effort of getting up and putting on his shoes and walking the hundred yards to the mess hall had to be weighed in the balance. "Thanks. I'll just lie right here," he said. "Any news of your boys?" he asked.

"Yes," said Whitejack. "The squadron came in."

"That's good."

"All except one plane." Whitejack sat down on the end of Stais' cot. His voice was soft and expressionless, under the bright electric light. "Johnny Moffat's plane."

In all the months that Stais had been in the air force, on fields to which planes had failed to return, he had learned that there was nothing to say. He was only nineteen years old, but he had learned that. So he lay quiet.

"They got separated in clouds on the way out of Ascension, and they never picked them up again. There's still a chance," Whitejack said, "that they'll drop in any minute." He looked at his watch. "Still a chance for another hour and forty minutes . . ."

There was still nothing to say, so Stais lay silent.

"Johnny Moffat," said Whitejack, "at one time looked as

though he was going to marry my sister. In a way, it's a good thing he didn't. It'd be a little hard, being brothers-in-law, on some of the parties the air force goes on in one place and another." Whitejack fell silent, looked down at his belly. Deliberately, he let his belt out a notch. He pulled it to, with a severe little click. "That fried chicken was mighty good," he said. "You sure you want to pass it up?"

"I'm saving my appetite," Stais said, "for my mother's cooking."

"My sister," said Whitejack, "was passing fond of Johnny, and I have a feeling when he gets home from the war and settles down, she's going to snag him. She came to me right before I left and she asked me if I would let her have ten acres on the north side of my property and three acres of timber to build their house. I said it was OK with me." He was silent again, thinking of the rolling ten acres of upland meadow in North Carolina and the three tall acres of standing timber, oak and pine, from which it would be possible to build a strong country house. "There's nobody in the whole world I'd rather have living on my property than Johnny Moffat. I've known him for twenty years and I've had six fist fights with him and won them all, and been alone with him in the woods for two months at a time, and I still say that. . . ." He got up and went over to his own cot, then turned and came back. "By the way," he said softly, "this is between you and me, Sergeant."

"Sure," said Stais.

"My sister said she'd murder me for my hide and taller if I ever let Johnny know what was in store for him." He grinned a little. "Women're very confident in certain fields," he said. "And I never did tell Johnny, not even when I was so drunk I was singing 'Casey Jones' naked in the middle of the city of

Tampa at three o'clock in the morning." He went over to his musette bag and got out a cigar and thoughtfully lit it. "You'd be surprised," he said, "how fond you become of nickel cigars in the Army."

"I tried smoking," said Stais. "I think I'll wait until I get a little older."

Whitejack sat heavily on his own cot. "Do you think they'll send you out to fight again?" he asked.

Stais stared up at the ceiling. "I wouldn't be surprised," he said. "There's nothing really wrong with me. I'm just tired."

Whitejack nodded, smoking slowly. "By the way," he said, "you heard us talking about the Lieutenant, didn't you?"

"Yes."

"I went out to the field and had a little conversation with him. He's just been sittin' there all day and most of the night since we got here, outside the Operations room, just lookin' and starin' across at the planes comin' in. Him and me, we've been good friends for a long time and I asked him pointblank. I said, 'Freddie,' I said, 'there's a question the boys're askin' themselves these days about you.' And he said, 'What's the matter?' And I said, 'The boys're asking if you've turned bad. You pass 'em and you don't even look at them as though you recognize 'em. What is it, you turn GI after a year?' I said. He looked at me and then he looked at the ground and he didn't say anything for maybe a minute. Then he said, 'I beg your pardon, Arnold. It never occurred to me.' Then he told me what was on his mind." Whitejack looked at his watch, almost automatically, then lifted his head again. "Ever since we got the order to go overseas he's been worrying. About the waist gunner and his navigator."

"What's he worrying about?" For a moment a crazy list of

all the thousand things you can worry about in the crew of one airplane flashed through Stais' head.

"They're not fighting men," Whitejack said slowly. "They're both good fellers, you wouldn't want better, but the Lieutenant's been watchin' 'em for a long time on the ground, in the air, at their guns, and he's convinced they won't measure. And he feels he's responsible for taking the Mitchell in and getting it out with as many of us alive as possible and he feels the waist gunner and the navigator're dangerous to have in the plane. And he's makin' up his mind to put in a request for two new men when we get to India, and he can't bear to think of what it'll do to the gunner and the navigator when they find out he's asked to have 'em grounded, and that's why he just sits there outside Operations, not even seein' us when we go by. . . ." Whitejack sighed. "He's twenty-two years old, the Lieutenant. It's a strain, something like that, for a man twenty-two years old. If you see Novak, you won't tell him anything, will you?"

"No," said Stais.

"I suppose things like this come up all the time in any army."

"All the time," said Stais.

Whitejack looked at his watch. Outside there was the growing and lapsing roar of engines that had been the constant sound of both their lives for so many months.

"Ah," said Whitejack, "they should've put me in the infantry. I can hit a rabbit at three hundred yards with a rifle, they put me in the Air Force and give me a camera. . . . Well, Sergeant, I think it's about time you were movin'."

Slowly, Stais got up. He put on his shoes and put his shaving kit into his musette bag and slung it over his shoulder.

"You ready?" asked Whitejack.

"Yes," said Stais.

"That all the baggage you got—that little musette bag?"

"Yes," said Stais. "I was listed as missing, presumed dead, and they sent all my stuff into the supply room and all my personal belongings home to my mother."

Stais looked around the barracks. It shone in the harsh army light of barracks at night all over the world, by now familiar, homelike, to all the men who passed through them. He had left nothing.

They walked out into the soft, engine-filled night. A beacon flashed nervously across the sky, dimming the enormous pale twinkle of Southern stars for a moment. They walked slowly, stepping cautiously over the ditches dug for the flood rains of the African West Coast.

As they passed the Operations room, Stais saw a young lieutenant slumped down in a wobbly old wicker chair, staring out across the field.

"They come yet?" Whitejack asked.

"No," said the lieutenant, without looking up.

Stais went into the building and into the room where they had the rubber raft and the patented radio and the cloth painted blue on one side and yellow on the other. A fat middle-aged ATC captain wearily told them about ditching procedure. There were more than thirty people in the room, all passengers on Stais' plane. There were two small, yellow Chinese who were going to be airsick and five bouncing fat Red Cross women, and three sergeants with a lot of Air Force medals, trying not to seem excited about going home, and two colonels in the Engineers, looking too old for this war. Stais only half listened as the fat captain explained how to inflate the raft, what strings to pull, what levers to move, where to find the waterproofed Bible. . . .

Whitejack was standing outside when Stais started for his plane. He gave Stais a slip of paper. "It's my home address," he said. "After the war, just come down sometime in October and I'll take you hunting."

"Thank you very much," said Stais gravely. Over Whitejack's shoulder he saw the lieutenant, still slumped in the wicker chair, still staring fixedly and unrelievedly out across the dark field.

Whitejack walked out to the great plane with Stais, along the oil-spattered concrete of the runway, among the Chinese and loud Red Cross women and the sergeants. They stopped, without a word, at the steps going up to the doorway of the plane and the other passengers filed past them.

They stood there, silently, with the two days of random conversation behind them and Brazil and Athens behind them, and five hundred flights behind them, and Jerusalem and Miami behind them, and the girls from Vienna and the American Embassy and Flushing, Long Island, behind them, and the Greek mountaineers behind them and Thomas Wolfe's funeral, and friends burning like torches, and dogs under treed raccoons in the Blue Ridge Mountains behind them, and a desperate twenty-two year old lieutenant painfully staring across a dusty airfield for ten days behind them, and the Mediterranean and the hospital bed in Cairo and Johnny Moffat wandering that night over the Southern Atlantic, with ten acres of meadow and three acres of timber for his house, and Whitejack's sister waiting for him, all behind them. And, ahead of Stais, home and a mother who had presumed him dead and wept over his personal belongings, and ahead of Whitejack the cold bitter mountains of India and China and the tearing dead sound of the fifties and the sky full of Japs. . . .

"All right, Sergeant," the voice of the lieutenant checking the passengers. "Get on."

Stais waved, a little broken wave, at Whitejack standing there. "See you," he said, "in North Carolina."

"Some October." Whitejack smiled a little, in the light of the floodlamps.

The door closed and Stais sat down in the seat in front of the two Chinese.

"I think these planes are absolutely charming," one of the Red Cross women was saying loudly. "Don't you?"

The engines started and the big plane began to roll. Stais looked out of the window. A plane was landing. It came slowly into the light of the runway lamps and set down heavily, bumping wearily. Stais stared. It was a Mitchell. Stais sighed to himself. As the big C54 wheeled at the head of the runway, then started clumsily down, Stais put the slip of paper with Arnold Whitejack written on it, and the address, in scrawling, childlike handwriting, into his pocket. And as he saw the Mitchell pull to a stop near the Operations room, he felt for the moment a little less guilty for going home.

WALKING WOUNDED

He wondered what had happened to the curtains. He lay stiffly on the bed, listening, with the old irritated tightening of the nerves, to the wild and grating hubbub of the Cairo street outside his window, the insane wailing of newsboys, the everlasting iron drip of garry-horses' hooves, the pained yelps of peddlers. The sun, bright and hurtful as hot nickel, cut in through the open windows. On the floor lay the curtains, torn, with bits of cord still running from them to the top of the windows, like a ruptured spider web.

"What happened to the curtains?" he asked. His voice felt dry and sandy in his throat and the right side of his head began to ache.

Mac was shaving at the washstand. His beard made a crinkly, Spartan sound against the razor. "Last night," Mac said, without turning. "In the excitement."

"What excitement?"

"You pulled the curtains down."

"Why?"

Mac shaved quietly and intently around the short, soldierly mustache. "Don't know," he said. "Either you wanted to throw me out, or throw yourself out, or just tear down the curtains."

"Oh, God!"

Mac scrubbed his face with water. "Pretty drunk, Peter," he said.

"What else did I do?"

"Two lieutenants and a major. In the lounge. Ten minutes of insults."

"A major! Christ!" Peter closed his eyes.

"I think you hit a lieutenant." Mac's voice was muffled in a towel. "Anyway, you hit something. Your hand's all cut up."

Peter opened his eyes and looked at his hand. Across the back of it, there was a wide, ugly wound, just beginning to puff up around the edges. As he looked at it, he realized that it was hurting him.

"I poured iodine over it," Mac said. "You won't die."

"Thanks." Peter let his hand drop, licked his dry lips. "What did I say to the major?"

" 'Base wallah.' 'Imperial vulture.' 'Gezira bloodsucker.' 'Headquarters hangman.' "

"That's enough." The right side of Peter's head hurt very strongly for a moment.

"You were a little unfair," Mac said calmly. "He was a nice type. Been in the desert three years. Just come back from Sicily with dysentery. Wounded twice. Been attached to headquarters four days."

"Oh, Christ," Peter said. "Oh, Christ."

The room was silent as Mac put on his shirt and combed his hair.

"Get his name?" Peter asked finally.

"Major Robert Lewis. Might be a good idea to say good morning."

"How about the lieutenants?"

Mac took out his notebook. "MacIntyre and Clark," he read. "They await your pleasure."

Peter sat up and swung his legs over the side of the bed.

The room faded and glittered for a moment and he had to hold on to the bed when he stood up.

"Some day, soon," he said, "I have to stop drinking."

"A little whisky," Mac said kindly, "is good for the soul. Anything I can do for you?"

"No, thanks."

Mac stood at the door.

"Mac . . ."

"Yes, Captain . . . ?" Tiny, astringent, helpful mockery in the title.

"Mac, this is the first time anything like this ever happened to me."

"I know," Mac said softly. He went quietly out of the room.

Peter walked slowly over to the wash basin, looked at himself in the mirror. The familiar long, thin face, the uneven dotted crenelation of his wound across his forehead, the strange dark mark in the eye that had been blind for three weeks, all seeming to tremble slightly now in the bitter sunlight, as it had trembled for two months.

He shaved carefully and went to take a shower. He came back, feeling better, and put on fresh clothes. He switched his tabs with the three pips to his clean shirt, looking absently and automatically to see if there was any lipstick on them. Three and a half years ago, at Arras, there had been lipstick one morning, and he had walked around all day long, ignorant, wondering why smiles hid on sergeants' lips.

Then he went down to apologize to the major.

He sat at his desk, sweating. The heat of Egypt was like the inside of a balloon. The balloon was being constantly filled; the pressure getting greater and greater. Typewriters clicked drily in the swelling air, and flies, the true owners of Egypt, whirled cleverly and maliciously before his eyes.

Sergeant Brown, his thick glasses clouded with sweat, clumped in and put a stack of papers on his desk, clumped out again. The back of Sergeant Brown's shirt was soaked where he had been pressing against the back of a chair, and sweat ran in trickles down his infantryman legs to the heavy wool socks and gaiters.

Peter stared at the stack of papers. Ruled forms and tiny and intricate notations that had to be gone over slowly, corrected, signed.

Outside, a donkey brayed painfully. It sounded like an immense wooden machine, in agony, wood grating against wood, incredibly loud. It made the little, paper-stacked room seem hotter than ever.

Peter re-read the letter he had received that morning from Italy. ". . . I am taking the liberty of answering your letter to Col. Sands, who was badly wounded last week. I am afraid there is nothing we can do about requesting your being posted to this regiment, as there is no provision in our establishment for medically graded officers."

The donkey brayed again outside. It sounded like the death of all the animals of Egypt on this hot morning.

Peter stared at the papers on his desk. Three flies danced over them, lighted, swept off. The typewriters rattled flatly in the heat. He took the top paper off the pile, looked at it. The figures leapt and wavered in the heat and a drop of sweat fell from his forehead and mistily covered a 3, a 7, an 8. His hands glistened in little sick beads and the paper felt slippery under his fingers. Hobnails sounded on the marble floor in the corridor, ostentatious and over-military among the clerks and filing cabinets. His throat burned drily with the fifteenth cigarette of the morning.

He stood up jerkily and took his hat and went out. In the corridor he passed Mrs. Burroughs. She was a tall, full-bodied girl who wore flowered prints and always seemed to manage silk stockings. She was going home to England to divorce her husband, who was a lieutenant in India. She was going to marry an American air-force major who had been switched to London from Cairo. She was very pretty and she had a soft, hesitant voice, and her bosom was always oppressively soft and noticeable under the flowered prints.

She smiled at him, hesitant, polite, gentle. She had two rosebuds clasped in her dark hair. "Good morning," she said, stopping, her voice cool, shy, inviting in the drab corridor. She always tried to stop him, talk to him.

"Good morning," Peter said stiffly. He never could look squarely at her. He looked down. No silk stockings this morning. The pretty legs bare, the skin firm and creamy. He had a sudden, hateful vision of Mrs. Burroughs landing in London, running to be crushed in the arms of the American major in the press of Waterloo Station, her eyes bright with tears of love and gratitude, her husband, used and forgotten, in India . . .

"I'm going to Groppi's," he heard himself say, surprisingly. "Tea. Would you like to join me?"

"Sorry," Mrs. Burroughs said, her voice sounding genuinely sorry. "So much work. Some other time. I'd be delighted . . ."

Peter nodded awkwardly, went out. He hated Mrs. Burroughs.

The street was full of heat, beggars, dirt, children with fly-eaten eyes, roaring army lorries. He put on his hat, feeling his forehead, wet and warm, rebel under the wool. A drunken New Zealander, at eleven o'clock in the morning, wobbled sorrowfully in the full glare of the sun, hatless, senseless, reft of dignity, 7,000 miles from his green and ordered island.

Groppi's was cooler, dark and shaded. The red-fezzed waiters in the long white gaballiehs moved quietly through the pleasant gloom. Two American sergeants with gunners' wings on their shirts solemnly were drinking two ice-cream sodas apiece.

Peter had tea and read the morning paper. The birth rate had gone up in England and an American magazine had suggested that Princess Elizabeth marry an American. The *Egyptian Mail* reprinted it with approval in a flood of Anglo-American feeling. After six years, somebody said in Parliament, men in the forces were to be sent home. The Russians were pouring across the Dnieper. Peter always saved the Russian news for last. Every step the Russians took was that much nearer home, nearer the rugged and manly weather of Scotland, nearer Anne . . .

He tried to think of Anne, what she looked like, what her skin felt like. He looked up at the ceiling and half closed his eyes to shut out the tea and ice-cream shop, to close out Egypt, summer, war, army, distance, absence, close out everything but his wife. But he couldn't remember what she looked like. He remembered the dress she wore when they were married and the inn they'd stayed at after Dunkirk and what they'd played at the concert the last night in London, and he remembered that he loved her. But her face, the sound of her voice . . . Lost. She refused to have photographs taken of her. Some whim or female superstition, far away in England . . .

He paid and went out and started back to his office. But

when he stood in front of the peeling, ornately balconied, sandbagged building and thought of the small, hot office, the endless papers, the sweat and hobnails, he couldn't go in. He turned and walked slowly down the street. He looked at his watch. Still an hour before the bars opened. He walked on the shady side, erect and soldierly, slowly, like a man with a grave purpose. A horribly dirty woman with a horribly dirty child, as dirty and street-worn as only Egyptians can be, followed him, whining, for half a block. Peter didn't walk any faster, although he felt his nerves jerking at the sound of the woman's voice.

The woman left him finally, and he walked deliberately through the crowded streets, stopping from time to time to peer into shop windows. French perfume, women's dresses, mangoes, books, photographs, his mind recorded heavily. He went into the photographer's and had his picture taken, refusing to smile, looking soberly square into the camera, intimidating the photographer. He would send the picture to Anne. Three years. How long could a woman be expected to remember a man? His face would stare solemnly at her morning, noon, and night, crying, "Remember me, remember your husband . . ."

Out in the street again he resumed his grave pacing down the shady side of the street. Fifteen minutes more and the bars would open. He grinned crookedly to himself as he thought of his pose before the camera, frozen Scotch passion grimly and puritanically peering across three years and two oceans. Anne would probably giggle at the absurdly stern, accusing face.

"Officer, wanna lady, wanna lady?"

Peter looked down. A tiny, filthy ten-year-old boy, barefooted, in a torn, bag-like single garment, was smiling up at him conspiratorially, pulling at his blouse.

"French lady," the boy whispered wickedly. "Fine French lady."

Peter stared at him disbelievingly, then broke into a roar of laughter. The boy, after a moment of doubt, also laughed.

"No, thank you, sir," Peter said.

The boy shrugged, grinned up at him. "Officer," he said, "cigarette?"

Peter gave him a cigarette and lit it for him and the boy darted off, to try the French lady on a Polish corporal.

The bar had a nice beery smell and was dark and cool and the bartender drew eight glasses at a time, letting the foam settle whitely on the glass rims.

"The two lieutenants," Peter was saying, "were a little stuffy, but the major was fine."

"I knew he would be," Mac said. "I talked to him last night."

"I had breakfast with him," Peter waved for two more beers, "and he said he guessed he'd be doing the same thing himself if he had to hang around this town five months."

Mac comfortably drained his beer.

"The birth rate in England," Peter said, "has gone up. I read it in the *Mail* this morning. There're three million Englishmen out of the country and the birth rate's rocketing. . . ." He heard his own voice loud and angry and humorless. "How in the name of God do they dare print things like that?" He saw Mac grinning widely, but he couldn't stop. "Who're the fathers? Where're the fathers? Bloody damned newspaper!"

"My," Mac said, "you have it bad today."

Suddenly Peter realized that Mac, placid and tolerant, was bearing a great deal of the burden of Peter's nerves.

"Mac," he said quietly, "Forgive me."

"Uh?" Mac looked at him, surprised.

"Wailing Wall Crome. Agony, Cairo division." Peter shook his head in disgust. "I keep feeding it to you seven days a week."

"Oh, shut up. I've lived with lots worse."

"Any time I get on your nerves, sing out, will you?"

"Sure thing. Drink your beer." Mac was embarrassed.

"I must be going a little crazy." Peter looked at his hands, which had taken to trembling in the last few months. The cigarette jerked minutely between his fingers, in a spasmodic rhythm. "This town. When I was with the regiment . . . Oh, hell . . ." The truth was that out in the desert, under the guns, on a pint of water a day, and the sudden air often dire with Stukas, he had been much happier. There were no women in the desert, no reminders of a civilized and normal life. There was clean, sterile sand, the noise of armor, thousands of grumbling, good-humored men intimate with an equal death, and above all there was the sense of immense and hardy effort and accomplishment, as first they had held the Afrika Corps and then driven it back. Cairo then had been a beautiful town, two days at a time, a hot bath and unlimited Scotch, and sweet clean sheets and relief from the guns. But now, under the dry flood of paper, under the stiffness and pettiness of headquarters politics, under the cheap weight of men who had clung to soft jobs for three years, with the streets full of bare-legged girls, with the war on another continent a thousand miles away . . .

Now the regiment, what was left of it, was broken up. Most

of them were in graves on the road to Tunis, others were in hospitals, the rest scattered among other units, after the four years that had started in France. Mac, who had been his platoon sergeant at Arras, calmly instructing the untrained men how to load and fire the guns they had never used before, then taking them out into the fresh May fields of France hunting for parachutists. Himself, who had crawled through the German lines to Dunkirk, who had entered Tripoli the first hour, who had blown up in the jeep outside Mareth, with his driver dead in the air beside him . . . Now, both of them clerks in small offices, chained to paper and civil servants.

"Six years," he said, "some bloody MP said we'd be sent home after six years. What do you think a woman thinks when she reads that she'll get her man back in only six years?"

"Always remember," Mac grinned, "what Monty said. 'The war can't last more than seven years. We'll run out of paper.'"

"If only I could get back to England," Peter said, "and sleep with my wife for two nights, everything would be all right. Just two nights."

Mac sighed. He was a quiet, efficient, small, matter-of-fact man, noticeably graying, and sighing was strange and incongruous to him. "Peter," he said, "can I talk plainly?"

Peter nodded.

"Peter, you ought to get yourself a girl."

They sat in silence. Peter played somberly with his beer. In France, even though he had just been married, he had been the gay young officer. Handsome and debonair, he had played joyfully and thoughtlessly with the pretty ladies of the country towns at which he'd been stationed, and in Paris, when he'd had a month there, a charming, beautifully dressed wife of a French captain stationed in Algiers.

But when he'd got back to England with the gray-faced remnants of his regiment, after the hideous, bloody days of the break-through and had taken his wife silently into his arms, all frivolity, all smallness and lack of faith had seemed wanton and irreligious in the face of so much ruin, such agony. Leaving England for Africa, he had felt that behind him he had to leave the best part of his life orderly and decent.

"Maybe," he said to Mac, "Maybe . . ."

"A man's got to be practical," Mac said. "Three years. Oh, my God!"

Peter had to smile at the drastic expression on the practical man's face.

"You'll just explode," Mac said, "and blow away."

Peter laughed loudly, nervously. "Whisky," he said, "provides certain compensations."

"Whisky," Mac said grimly, "will send you home a doddering wreck. You'll do no one any good that way."

"Maybe. Maybe . . ." Peter shrugged. "Anyway, I hate these women out here. Having the best time of their lives. Ugly, impossible girls no one would ever look at in peacetime, just because there are a hundred men for every woman . . . Snobbish, over-confident . . . Bitches, all of them. A man has to sacrifice all decent, male pride to chase after one of these . . ." He talked faster and faster, all the bitter observation of the past years flooding to his tongue. "They demand abasement, homage, the ugliest, horrible and meanest of them. Women," he said, "have been among the most horrible of the war's casualties. All humility's gone, all normal value, all friendship. They're man-greedy. They're profiteering on the war, like the worst usurer and manufacturer of machine-tools, except that their profits are lieutenants and generals, not cash. After the war," he said, "we should have rehabilitation hospitals for women who have been in troop areas, just like the hospitals for maimed men, to teach them how to live normal lives again . . ."

Mac was laughing by now, helplessly, into his beer. "Enough," he said. "Enough, John Knox! All I wanted to say is that I have a date tonight, and my girl has a friend who's just come from Jerusalem and it might do you a world of good just to have dinner with a woman for once. Do you want to go?"

Peter flushed, looked down at the beer-ringed table. "I won't even know how to talk to a woman any more."

"Do you want to go?"

Peter opened his mouth, closed it. "All right," he said. "All right."

"Jerusalem is nice enough . . ." It was on the dance floor at the Auberge des Pyramides, under the stars, with the three great tombs standing huge and a rebuke to time in the darkness just outside the lights and the music. Joyce was talking as they went slowly and painfully around the dance floor. "The city's clean, and the King David's an amusing hotel, but the people're simply dreadful." She had a brittle, drawling voice, pitched just high enough so that everyone near by could hear clearly what she was saying. "There," she said brightly, as Peter managed a full turn, "we're doing much better, aren't we?"

"Yes," Peter said, sweating in the heavy Nile heat, only slightly tempered by night, as he tried to concentrate on the beat of the music. Joyce's voice distracted him and put him off and somehow she never seemed to stop talking. She worked in the consular service and by nine-thirty Peter had a full store of information on the doings of the consulate in Jerusalem for the last year and a half, at which time Joyce had come out from England. He had hardly said a word all night, stammering, half finishing sentences, suffering, feeling like the clumsiest farmer. Still, she was pretty, most desirable in a full white evening gown ("We always dress in Jerusalem"), with full, sleek shoulders bare and daring under the gay lights.

"That's King Farouk. . . ." For the first time all evening her voice dropped a bit. "Isn't it?"

Peter looked. "Yes," he said.

"Isn't he attractive? What an original beard!"

Peter looked at King Farouk. "He looks like a fat, self-satisfied young man," Peter said, the first full sentence he had got out all evening. "And I understand he grew the beard because he has a terrible case of acne."

"Dance around the edge of the dance floor," Joyce whispered. "I'd like people to see me."

Dutifully and heavily Peter danced around the edge of the floor until the music stopped. He followed Joyce to the table. Joyce smiled vivaciously at seven or eight officers seated at various tables throughout the establishment.

"It's amazing," she said, brightly and loudly, "how many men I know in Cairo." They sat down. There was an awful silence while Peter wondered where in the name of God Mac was, and his girl, and Joyce smiled prettily first at one table, then another.

"Are you married?" Peter heard his voice, crooked and rasping, asking inexplicably. For the first time that evening Joyce gave him her undivided attention.

"Why," she said, looking at him queerly and coldly, "what a strange question!"

"It's just that there's a girl around my office," Peter said, almost dazedly. "Married to a lieutenant in India. Marrying an American major in London . . ." The expression on Joyce's face became more and more strained. "I don't know what made me think of her," Peter said lamely.

"No," Joyce said coldly, "I'm not married."

"I am," Peter said, despairingly.

"Really." Joyce smiled automatically at a colonel four tables away.

"My wife," said Peter, not knowing why he was talking, feeling his tongue too loose from the drinking that had been continuous since six that evening, "my wife is a woman of admirable character, although I can't remember what she looks like. Her name is Anne. She works for the Air Ministry in Manchester. After Dunkirk, I was stationed on the beach at Dover for five months. I used to manage to get away weekends. We'd just stay in one room and just look at each other. After France . . . I felt as though my wife had healed me of a dreadful disease. She healed me of mud and death and friends dying on all sides. She's most beautiful, but I don't remember what she looks like. She's very calm and simple and her voice is low, although I don't remember that, either. I sent her my photograph today. Six years is too long for a man to expect a woman to remember him. Someone ought to tell Parliament that . . . Don't you think?"

Joyce was staring at him, her mouth frozen to one side. "Yes," she said.

"If I could only see her for two nights . . ." Well, finally, the thought crossed his consciousness, the lady from Jerusalem is listening to me. "Right before I came out here, I was moved to another beach. It was raining. Autumn and miserable and barbed wire at the high-tide marks and mines all over the beaches. I called her long-distance and she told me she had a week and asked me if she should come down. I told her no. It was so miserable. Cheap little shacks waiting for the Germans in the rain. I knew we were leaving for Africa and I didn't want our last days together to be dreary, in that abominable place. I told her no, but she said, 'You wait right there. I'm coming down tonight.'" Suddenly, above the dance music in the Valley of the Nile, Peter remembered what his wife's voice had sounded like, merry and sensual and confidently commanding over the faulty wires on that autumn night on a wet beach on the English Channel. "She came down and we had the week together, and the rain and the barbed wire made no difference at all. I've never been so gay, and it was early in the war, and we always had a coal-fire and hot rum and lovely heavy breakfasts, with the curtains still drawn. And never a tear when she left. And I started for Africa singing in my heart." He was talking straight ahead to the pyramids in the ancient desert darkness now, not to the silly, bare-shouldered girl across the table. "I haven't heard from her in two months. Not a letter in two months." He shrugged. "After the war," he said, "I'm going to go in for politics. I'm going to stand for Parliament. There must be somebody in Parliament who knows what a war is like, who knows that one war is enough, six years is too much . . ."

"Why, Joyce, how nice!" It was the colonel, standing gallantly at the table. "Dance?"

Joyce looked doubtfully at Peter. Peter stood up, a little unsteadily. "Delighted," he said ambiguously. Without looking at Peter, Joyce went off with the colonel, smiling impartially at dozens of officers in Sam Browne belts as she danced on the edge of the floor.

Peter hazily watched the flashing plump white dress among the brave khaki and brass pips. He passed his hand over his eyes, thinking, as he remembered his outburst, God, I must be going crazy.

He saw a captain step in and dance with Joyce, then an American major. "The world," he said softly to himself, "is full of American majors." He laughed gently to himself, stood up, walked slowly out of the night club. Outside, with the music thin and distant in his ears, the Pyramids loomed, crumbling in the darkness, in memory of the unremembered dead.

He got into a cab and started for Cairo.

When the cab got to Gezira Island, he tapped the driver on the shoulder. "Sporting Club," he said.

The old, wheezing taxi laboriously turned. "I need a drink," Peter told himself seriously. "I need a drink very badly." He thought of old Mac caught there with two girls and the tremendous bill. He felt badly about it, but he'd pay his share, although it would mean considerably less drinking for the rest of the month. But he couldn't stay with that damned girl. The truth was he couldn't stay with any girl. Anne, unphotographed, in Manchester . . . Still, she should write more often than once every two months. . . .

The bar at Gezira was still open. There were some South Africans and some American fliers lounging against it. One of the American fliers was singing, in a soft Southern voice, "Oh, Susannah, don't you cry for me . . ."

"Scotch," Peter said to the bartender, feeling for the first time that evening, a cessation of loneliness, his constant climate.

"Fo' Ah'm gawn t' Alabama, with mah banjo on mah knee . . ." the American pilot sang sweetly and happily.

"Gin and lime," said one of the South Africans, a gigantic captain with huge bare arms, whom the others called Lee. "Gin and lime all around." He turned to Peter. "What're you drinking? Captain?"

"I've ordered, thanks." Peter smiled at him.

"Man says he's ordered," the American pilot sang. "What do you know about that? British captain says he's ordered. Order again and order again, oh Captain, order again . . ."

The bartender put two Scotches in front of Peter, grinning. The huge South African captain poured it all into one glass. They lifted their glasses.

"To South Africa," one of the Americans said.

They drank.

"To sergeants." The American who had been singing grinned at a large South African lieutenant with a mustache. The lieutenant looked around him uneasily. "Quiet, please," he said. "I'll be in jail five years."

"This gentlemen looks like a gentlemen." Lee put his arm around the lieutenant with the mustache. "Doesn't he?"

"Yes," said Peter.

"Jail," said the lieutenant with the mustache.

"He's not a gentleman. He is a sergeant. He is my bloody sergeant from my bloody company."

"Ten years," said the lieutenant with the mustache.

"We're all AWOL, Sergeant Monks, lieutenant for the evening, Lieutenant Fredericks . . ." He waved to a slightly smaller red-headed South African down the bar. "And myself. We're farmers. Independent men. When the bloody O.C. said 'no leaves,' we said farewell. Sixty miles out on the desert for three weeks. Miserable little clerk of an O.C. Sergeant, I said, here's a pip. Take off those bloody stripes. We wish to show you the glories of Shepheard's and Gezira, so that you can come back and dazzle the poor bastards in the other ranks with tales of the high life of Cairo."

"I've been talking to brigadiers all afternoon and evening," Monks complained. "Wearing on the nerves."

"If the O.C. shows up, it's all taped," Lee said. "I grab Monks by one arm, Freddy grabs him by the other. 'We've just arrested the bugger, sir,' we say. 'Impersonating an officer.' "

"Ten years," Monks said, grinning. "This round is on me."

Peter laughed. He lifted his glass. "To sergeants everywhere." They all drank.

"On my right," said Lee, "is the American Air Force."

The American Air Force raised its glasses at Peter and the pilot who sang started in on "Chattanooga Choo-choo." There were two lieutenants and a twenty-four-year-old major.

"The American Air Force is going home," said Lee. "Their tour is over. Home by way of England. The infantry's tour is never over. Oh, the poor, stinking, bloody infantry, their tour is never over . . ."

"Unskilled labor," one of the pilots said calmly. "We're delicate and highly sensitive mechanisms. We are war-weary. Our Schneiders are low as an Egyptian whore. We've bombed too many places. We've seen too much flak. We are lopsided from wearing ribbons. We are going home now to instruct the young how to shoot."

"I am going home to play with my wife," the twenty-four-year-old major said soberly.

"The infantry is not under the same Awful Strain," said the pilot who had been singing. "All they have to do is walk in and be shot. Their nerves are not stretched to the breaking point like ours. Captain," he said, leaning back and talking to Peter, "you look a little war-weary yourself."

"I'm pretty war-weary," Peter said.

"He looks sensitive," the major said. "He looks fine and sensitive enough to be at least a navigator. He looks like Hamlet on a rough night."

"I was in the tanks," Peter said.

"It's possible," said the major, "to get war-weary in a tank, too, I suppose."

"It's possible," Peter said, grinning.

". . . breakfast in Carolina . . ." sang the musical pilot.

"When're you leaving for home?" Peter asked.

"6 A.M. tomorrow. 0600 hours, as they say in the army," said the major.

"Five or six glorious days in London among our brave English Allies and cousins," said the other pilot, "and then the Stork Club, the Harvard-Yale football game, all the blonde, full-bosomed, ribbon-conscious, lascivious American girls . . ."

"London," said Peter. "I wish I were going with you."

"Come along," said the major expansively. "We have a nice empty Liberator. Pleased to have you. Closer relations with our British comrades. Merely be at the airport at 0600 hours, as they say in the army."

"Did you see," asked the singing pilot, "in the *Mail* today? Some idiot wants Princess Elizabeth to marry an American."

"Excellent idea," said the major. "Some upstanding representative citizen of the Republic. Post-war planning on all fronts. My nomination for Prince Escort is Maxie Rosenbloom."

Everyone considered the suggestion gravely.

"You could do worse," the pilot said.

"Infusion of sturdy American stock into an aging dynasty,"

the major said. "The issue would be strongly built, with good left hands . . ."

"Do you mean it?" Peter asked. "You really could take me?"

"Delighted," the Major said.

The singing pilot started in on "All Alone," and everyone but Peter joined him. Peter stared unseeingly at the glasses and bottles behind the bar. In three days he could be home. Three days and he could walk into Anne's room, quietly, unannounced, smiling a little tremulously as she looked up unsuspectingly. Maybe it was possible. He had had no leave since he'd come to Africa, except for two weeks' convalescent. He could go immediately to Colonel Foster's apartment, explain to him. Colonel Foster liked him, was very sympathetic. If he gave him a written order, releasing him from duty for twenty-one days, he, Peter, would undertake to get transportation back. Somehow, somehow . . . He would take all the responsibility himself. He was sure that Colonel Foster, who was a good soul, would do it.

Peter stood up straight. He spoke to the American major. "Perhaps I'll see you at six o'clock."

"Fine," the major said heartily. "It's going to be a great trip. We're loaded with Scotch." He waved as Peter turned and left the bar.

"All alone, by the telephone . . ." the wailing, mocking voices quavered in the night. Peter got into a taxicab and gave Colonel Foster's address.

He felt he was trembling. He closed his eyes and leaned back. It was all absolutely possible. England was only three days away. Two weeks there and the desert and the guns and the dying and ruled paper and heat and loneliness and insane expanding tension would disappear. He could face the rest of the war calmly, knowing that he would not explode, would not lose his reason. It was possible. Men were going home to their wives. That American major. All so cheerful and matter-of-fact about it. England in three days, after the three years . . . Colonel Foster would most certainly say yes. Peter was sure of it as the taxi drove up to the dark building where Colonel Foster lived. Peter paid the driver and looked up. The colonel's window was alight, the only one in the entire building. Peter felt his breath coming fast. It was a symbol, an omen. The man was awake. His friend, who could give him England tonight with five strokes of a pen, by luck was wakeful in the quiet night, when all the rest of the city slept around him. It would be irregular, and Colonel Foster would be running some risk, but he had rank enough and was independent enough to take the chance. . . .

Peter rang the night-bell to the side of the locked doors of the apartment building. Far in the depths of the sleeping stone and brick, a forlorn and distant bell sang weirdly.

As he waited for the hall-boy to open the doors, Peter hastily rehearsed his story. No leave in three years. The tension getting worse and worse. Medically graded, no chance of getting to an active unit. Regiment disbanded. Work deteriorating. Given to sudden fits of temper and what could only be described as melancholia, although a doctor wouldn't believe it until it was too late. He knew the British Army couldn't provide transportation, but here were these Americans with an empty Liberator. He'd get back somehow.

As he went over it, in the darkness, with the far-away bell sounding as though it were ringing at the bottom of a troubled sea, Peter was sure the logic was irrefutable; Foster couldn't refuse.

When the hall-boy finally opened the door, Peter sprang past him, raced up the steps, too impatient to take the elevator.

He was panting when he rang Colonel Foster's bell, and the sweat was streaming down the sides of his face. He rang the bell sharply, twice. He heard his breath whistling into his lungs, and he tried to compose himself, so that Colonel Foster would think him absolutely calm, absolutely lucid . . .

The door opened. The figure at the door was silhouetted against the yellowish light behind it.

"Colonel," Peter said, panting, "I'm so glad you're up. I must talk to you. I hate to disturb you, but . . ."

"Come in." The door was opened wider and Peter strode down the hall, into the living room. He heard the door close and turned around. "I . . ." he began. He stopped. The man who was standing there was not Colonel Foster. It was a large, red-faced man, bald, in a tattered red bathrobe. He had a mustache and tired eyes and he was holding a book in his hand. Peter looked at the book. *The Poems of Robert Browning.*

The man stood there, waiting, pulling his bathrobe a little tighter, a curious little smile on his weary face.

"I . . . I saw the light, sir," Peter said. I thought Colonel Foster would be up and I took the liberty of . . . I had some business with . . ."

"Colonel Foster doesn't live here," the man said. His voice was clipped and military, but tired, aging. "He moved out a week ago."

"Oh," Peter said. He suddenly stopped sweating. He swallowed, made a conscious effort to speak quietly. "Do you know where he lives, sir?"

"I'm afraid not. Is there anything I can do, Captain? I'm

Colonel Gaines." He smiled, false teeth above the old robe. "That's why when you said Colonel, at the door, I . . ."

"No, sir," Peter said. "Nothing, sir. I'm dreadfully sorry. This time of night . . ."

"Oh, that's all right." The man waved a little embarrassedly. "I never go to sleep. I was reading."

"Well . . . Thank you, sir. Good night."

"Uh . . ." the man looked hesitantly at him, as though he felt that somehow Peter should be helped in some dubious, obscure way. "Uh—perhaps a drink. I have some whisky I was just going to—for myself . . ."

"No, thank you, sir," Peter said. "I'd better be getting along."

Clumsily, they went down the passage together to the door. The man opened the door. He stood there, red-faced, huge, British, like a living Colonel Blimp, lonely and tired, with Robert Browning in the foreign night.

"Good night, sir."

"Good night . . ."

The door closed and Peter walked slowly down the dark stairs.

Peter started toward his hotel, but the thought of the disordered room and Mac lying there, steadily asleep, steadily and slightly snoring in the next bed, was impossible.

He walked slowly past the dark policemen standing quietly with their rifles on the street corners. Down the street garry-lights, small and flickering and lonesome, wandered past and the sound of the horses' hooves was deliberate and weary.

He came to the English Bridge and stood on the banks of the river, looking at the dark water swirling north toward the Mediterranean. Down the river a felucca, its immense sail spread in a soaring triangle, slowly made its way among the shadows from the trees along the shore. Across the river a minaret, poignant with faith, shone sharp and delicate in the moonlight.

Peter felt spent and drained. A nervous and hysteric pulse pulled at his bad eye and a gigantic sob seemed wedged into his throat.

Overhead, far away, there was the sound of a plane. It came nearer, passed across the stars, died away, going somewhere.

The wedge dislodged and the sob broke out like tears and blood.

Peter closed his eyes and when he opened them again the wild pulse had stopped, his throat was clear. He stared across the river at the minaret, faithful and lovely in the light of the moon, by the side of the old river.

Tomorrow, he thought, tomorrow there may be a letter from home . . .

HAMLETS OF THE WORLD

The Captain was getting more and more remote every moment. He kept stuffing papers into a heavy saddle-leather bag, whistling tunelessly under his breath. From time to time he looked out over the windy plain, swirling with dust in the late afternoon sun. He would peer thoughtfully into the eye-burning distance, then shake himself a little and resume his packing, a little more quickly each time. He never looked at Lieutenant Dumestre.

Lieutenant Dumestre sat on the edge of the desk, very neat in his expensive uniform. He was a tall, fairish man, who looked too young to be in his lieutenant's uniform, too young to be so serious, too young to be in a war.

He never took his eyes off the Captain. The Captain was a round, solid man, who had been very jovial when they had met in Algiers and had paid for the wine and had sighed gallantly over all the pretty women in the café. There was nothing jovial or gallant about the Captain now, as he prepared in a businesslike way to disappear, each moment seeming more and more remote.

"Do you expect to come back, sir?" Lieutenant Dumestre finally asked, because the silence in the orderly room broken only by the low bumble of the captain's humming was at last too much to bear.

The Captain stopped his packing and looked thoughtfully

out over the plain again, as though there, in the dust and scrub, some answer to a profound although somewhat vague question was to be found. He stood silently, even forgetting to hum.

"Do you expect to come back, sir?" the Lieutenant asked loudly.

The Captain at last turned and looked at the Lieutenant. His eyes were very cool and you would never have thought from looking at him in this moment that he had ever bought a bottle of wine for a lieutenant in his life. "Come back?" the Captain said. He turned away and sturdily buckled his bag. "Who can tell?"

"What do I do with the Americans?" The Lieutenant's voice, he noticed angrily, was much higher than it should have been. At Saint Cyr they had been after him all the time to pitch his voice lower. "An order given in the soprano register, Mister, is not calculated to drive troops to impossible glories." "What happens when the Americans arrive?"

The Captain was putting his helmet on very carefully in front of a mirror. "That is just what I hope to discover," he said.

"In the meantime?"

"In the meantime your orders are to resist. Naturally."

The Lieutenant peered out over the plain, hoping painfully that over the rim of the horizon the Americans would appear before the Captain could leave on his personal retreat. But the only movement to be seen was a corporal hurrying to the battery observation post.

"They'll arrive tomorrow morning, at the latest," the Lieutenant said.

"Quite possibly." The Captain picked up his bag decisively, marched out and into the command car. The Lieutenant followed him and saluted. The Captain saluted and the car started and the Captain drove down the road.

The Lieutenant plodded slowly up the road toward the forward gun, thinking of the Captain, in the command car, speeding over a macadam road to Algiers, where there would be other men to make the decisions, other men to say, "We will move to the left, we will move to the right . . ." and the Captain would have to make no decisions himself. No matter how things turned out, he would not be committed and would be a fine fellow with whichever side turned up on top, and would jovially buy wine for his new lieutenants at the second-best restaurant in town. . . .

The Lieutenant made his way to the aimless little mud house they used as an observation post and climbed the ladder and stood under the umbrella next to the red-eyed little corporal and peered through his glasses at the plain. He looked until his eyes ached, but aside from the blowing dust there was nothing.

The men who served the forward gun had rigged up a tarpaulin to one side and lay under it, out of the wind. Usually they slept all the afternoon, but today no one was sleeping.

Sergeant Fourier even went so far as to get up and look out across the plain.

"Anything?" Labat asked.

The Sergeant squinted anxiously. "Nothing."

"Waiting, everything is waiting," Labat said. He was a long, ugly man, with a big nose and large ears. He was from Paris and excitable and given to throwing his arms around in rage and was a great patriot of the French Republic. "In a war you wait for everything! Even the Americans! At last, I thought, things will finally move. The Americans are famous for their briskness. . . . We're still waiting. . . ."

"Only a day," said Boullard. Boullard was a big, quiet man, over forty, with a wrinkled, brown, farmer's face. "They'll be here soon enough."

"I can't wait," Labat said. He stood up and peered out. "For a year I sat in the Maginot Line. Now for two years I sit here. I am finally impatient. A day is too much."

"Shut up," Boullard said calmly. "You'll get us all nervous."

Labat lay down and put his hands behind his head and looked up at the tarpaulin angrily. Sergeant Fourier came back and sat down.

"More of the same," Sergeant Fourier said. "More nothing."

"It must be worse for Americans," Corporal Millet said. He was a man who, although he was nearly thirty-five, was still plagued by pimples. His face had raging red blots on it all the time and he suffered meanly under his affliction, taking his misfortune out on the work details in his charge. "It must be unbearable for Americans."

"Why?" Labat asked angrily. "What's wrong with the Americans?"

"They are not a military people," Corporal Millet said. He had a lawyer's voice, smooth and reasonable and superior, and on bad days it made men want to kill Corporal Millet. "They are used to sitting back and pushing buttons."

"Corporal," Labat said calmly, "you are perhaps the biggest idiot in the French Army of 1942."

"The jokes," Corporal Millet said. "We can do without the jokes. It is a fact that war is harder on some races than on others. The Americans must be suffering the tortures of the damned."

"I repeat," Labat said. "The biggest."

Corporal Millet was a devotee of Vichy, and Labat enjoyed making him angry.

"Push buttons," Boullard said reflectively. "I could use a few push buttons at the moment."

"See," Corporal Millet gestured to Boullard. "Boullard agrees."

"See," Boullard said. "Boullard does not agree."

There was silence for a moment, while the men thought of the wind and the ugliness of the men around them and the possibility of dying tomorrow.

"This war," the Sergeant said. "This disease of a war."

"Somebody talk about a woman," Private Jouvet said. "I'm tired of the war. I am in the mood for breasts and hips." Private Jouvet was twenty years old and made a desperate effort to keep on an equal footing with these sun-stricken veterans of bed and battle.

"It can't be," Labat said, "that the Americans will appear and we will be asked to shoot at them. It's impossible."

"In the French Army," Boullard said, "nothing is impossible."

"Why not?" Corporal Millet asked in his bland voice. "An invasion of French soil . . ."

"I am very tired of those two words," Boullard said. "French soil."

Labat opened his canteen and took a mouthful. He closed the canteen over the precious water and then thought that perhaps he would be shot by morning, and said, "Hell," and opened the canteen and took another mouthful.

"The problem is," Private Jouvet said, "are the Americans to be regarded as friends, enemies, or tourists?"

"What a war!" Sergeant Fourier sighed. He had just married three months before, a masseuse with a good clientele in Algiers, and he was by and large as comfortable as a sergeant could hope to be in this foul year. "What a disease of a war!"

"Lafayette," Boullard said, "we are here."

"We will be given our orders," Corporal Millet said loudly.

"That's what we're afraid of," said Labat.

"After all," said Corporal Millet, tenderly touching his current most blazing pimple, "we are soldiers. We have officers. They have their instructions."

"Please, Colonel," said Labat. "Quiet. Such official sentiments have a tendency to make me throw up."

"The Americans," Sergeant Fourier sighed again. "Things were going as well as could be expected. This wasn't good, but a man could bear it. They are crazy with anxiety to make a landing some place. . . . They have all Europe to make a landing on. No! They must choose Africa! We will all be dead."

"Be more cheerful," Boullard said, "or kindly keep quiet."

The men sat silently for a moment, everyone heavy and gloomy because the word death had finally been mentioned.

"It will be a ridiculous thing," Labat said. "To be killed by an American." Labat had fought at Sedan and made his way bitterly down the length of France, cursing the politicians, cursing the officers, cursing the Germans and English and Italians and Americans. At last he had stowed away aboard a freighter to Algiers and without losing a day had joined up all over again and had since then sat, full of pent-up vengeance, in the gloom of Africa, waiting to fight the Germans once more.

"I refuse," Labat said. "I refuse to be killed by an American."

"You will be told what your orders are," Corporal Millet said, "and you will follow them."

Labat stared gloomily and dangerously at Corporal Millet.

His face which was ugly but usually pleasant enough now was harsh and his eyes were squinted balefully. "Corporal," he said, "Corporal of the pimples, do you know what our orders are?"

"No."

"Does anybody know?" Labat looked around, his face still flushed and glowering, angry at Corporal Millet and the government of France and his position in the world that afternoon.

Sergeant Fourier cleared his throat professionally. "The Lieutenant. He must know. The Captain's gone . . ."

"What a wonderful thing," Boullard said, "to be a captain. . . ."

"Let us ask the Lieutenant," Labat said.

"Sergeant Fourier, we make you a committee of one."

Sergeant Fourier looked around him uneasily, pulling in his round little belly nervously, uncomfortable at the thought of any action that would make him conspicuous, endanger his pleasant anonymous future with the masseuse in Algiers. "Why me?" he asked.

"Highest non-commissioned officer present," Labat chanted. "Channels of communication with the commissioned personnel."

"I haven't said two words to him," Sergeant Fourier protested. "After all, he just got here five days ago. And he's reserved. . . . All he's said to me in five days is, 'Make sure the men do not smoke in the open at night.' "

"Enough," Labat said cheerfully. "It's obvious he likes you."

"Don't joke," Boullard said sharply. "We have no more time to joke."

"I'm only joking," Labat said soberly, "because I am willing to slit my throat."

He got up and went to the edge of the tarpaulin and stood there, his back to the men, watching across the enigmatic plain for the first fateful dust cloud.

"What sort of man is this Lieutenant Dumestre?" Boullard asked.

"It's hard to tell," Sergeant Fourier said, with the caution born of three years in an army where a hasty approval of a man, before all the facts of courage, sense and rectitude were in, might one day cause your death. "He's very quiet. Stiff . . ."

"A bad sign," said Boullard.

"Very rich in the uniform department."

"Another bad sign."

"It doesn't pay to be too hurried," Sergeant Fourier protested.

"It's the Americans," Boullard said. "They're in a hurry, not me. Well, there's only one thing to be done." He rubbed his cheek absently with the back of his hand, like a man determining whether or not he needs a shave. The other men watched him silently, anxious and curious about a definite plan that might have finally bloomed on this last nervous afternoon. "One thing," Boullard repeated. "We kill him."

Lieutenant Dumestre stood in the observation post and felt the headache coming on like an express train. Every afternoon the boredom and misery of the day accumulated in his brain pan and punished him for still living. He stared painfully over the darkening plain, which was silently enveloping itself in blue and purple folds, intangible and deceptive, in which the shapes of men and machines might be capriciously and dangerously lost. . . .

Lieutenant Dumestre shook his head and closed his eyes, measuring gloomily the exact extent of the pain in his skull.

How do you do it? he asked himself. How does a first lieutenant hand a battery over to an advancing army, without orders? How does a first lieutenant save his life in a situation like this? In the distance there is a puff of dust and soon the first shell dropping somewhere near you, and all around you doubtful and uncertain men whom you do not know but who, for the lack of a better word, are under your command. Why had he left his post in Algiers? In this one, crazy fateful week, his transfer had to be granted, this transfer to dilemma, this transfer to death. . . . In the days of Napoleon it was said that every French private had a marshal's baton in his knapsack. Today every French soldier had in his knapsack a fatal and insoluble conundrum.

Lieutenant Dumestre had asked to be transferred from Algiers because he had been spending too much money there. It was as simple as that. The bills came in, the monthly reckonings were made, the deductions for the money sent home to his mother and father, who were lean and ailing in Paris, and it became clear that on a lieutenant's salary you could not save money in a gay town, especially if you had been rich all your life and your family rich before you and certain habits of eating and drinking and generosity ingrained in you, war or no war . . .

So, it was too expensive, Algiers. So, the desert would prove to be even more expensive.

. . . Back in Algiers he knew the men of his battery had mimicked him behind his back—his slow, painful way of delivering orders, full of agonized pauses, as he tried to remember to keep his voice down, tried not to sound like a young idiot imposing callously on these veterans of a war that had passed him by. . . . They had mimicked him, but he knew them and even felt they liked him and if he were with them now in this tragedy of a situation, he would be able to go to them, talk to them, draw strength and resolution, one way or another from the men who would have to bear the burden of living and dying with him.

But here he was, on the one important day of the last two years, with a group of sullen and bearded strangers, who regarded him only with steady and cool hostility, a newcomer and an officer in an army where newcomers were automatically suspect and officers automatically hated. . . .

Lieutenant Dumestre walked slowly out toward the west across the dusty scrub. The sun had set and the wind had died and the walking, he felt, might help somehow. Perhaps, he thought, smiling a little to himself, there will be an American patrol and I am unavoidably captured and there's an end to the problem . . . It's like a child, he thought, hoping that by morning he will have a sore throat so he does not have to go to school and take his examination in arithmetic. What an arithmetic was being imposed upon him now! What a savage and pitiless calculation! He looked toward the last blur of the horizon beyond which the Americans were marching. How simple it was to be an American! In their arithmetic there was an answer to all problems. How merry and dashing a lieutenant in the artillery in the American army must feel tonight, marching beside men whom he could trust, who trusted him, who all believed the same thing, who knew an enemy when they saw one, whose parents were well-fed and healthy, in no one's power, three thousand sweet miles from all battlefields. . . .

What a tragic thing to be a Frenchman this year! Hamlet, sword out, killing Polonius and uncle in blind unprofitable lunges. . . . Frenchmen, Hamlets of the world . . .

Lieutenant Dumestre stopped and sat down like a little boy on the dark earth and put his head in his hands and wept. He stopped suddenly and bit his lips and neglected to dry the tears from his cheeks. Nonsense, he thought, a grown man. . . . There must be an answer to this, too. After all, I am not the only Frenchman afloat on this continent. The thing is, the men. If I knew what they wanted . . . If there was only some way to be present, without being seen. Armies have surrendered before. Detachments have surrendered before. Officers have appeared under a flag of truce and offered their services to their official enemies. The Captain was in Algiers, there was no one to stop him. "Dear sir, is there anyone here who speaks French? Dear sir, Lieutenant Dumestre, Battery C, wishes to state that he desires to join forces with the American Army in North Africa and put himself under the flag of the United States for the duration against the common enemy . . ." There must be a technique to surrender, just the way there was a technique for everything else in the army. His mother and father would have to look out for themselves. Now, if only the men . . .

Lieutenant Dumestre slapped his thigh briskly as he stood up. At last he had reached a decision. He had faced the arithmetic and at least he knew what answer he wanted. There only remained going in frankly to the men and putting the situation up to them, in words of one syllable, simply. . . . He started back toward the forward gun, walking more swiftly than he had walked for a week.

"Men," he would say, remembering to keep his voice pitched low, "this is the way it is. You may or may not know it, but tomorrow an American army will appear." You never knew how much the men knew, what rumors had reached them, what facts confirmed, what punishments and discharges and prophecies and movements were peddled at the latrine or over a morning cigarette. "I am under orders to resist," he would say. "Personally, I do not believe we are bound by those orders, as I believe all Frenchmen to be on the side for which the Americans are now fighting." Perhaps that was too heroic, but it was impossible to fight a war without sounding from time to time a little heroic. "I intend to go out under a flag of truce and give over the guns of this battery." Now the question of dissenters. "Anyone who does not wish to join me in this action is free to leave toward the rear. . . ." No, they'd go back and talk and by morning a troop of cavalry would come up and Lieutenant Dumestre would be finished in thirty minutes. Keep them with him? How do that? Supposing they were all Vichy men? After all, they were being paid by Vichy and there were thousands of Frenchmen in Africa who had staked their lives on a German victory. They'd shoot him in cold blood.

Once more he cursed the trick that had landed him at this moment among two hundred strangers. In his old company he would have been able to take Sergeant Goubille aside and talk honestly and get an honest answer. Sergeant Goubille was forty-five years old and there was something fatherly and tolerant of young officers in his bearing, and a man like that would be worth a man's life on this harsh and doubtful plain tonight. Well, there was no Sergeant Goubille at hand. . . . Perhaps that Breton, that farmer, Boullard. He was an older man and he looked honest and pleasant.

He took a deep breath and walked swiftly, not knowing exactly what he would do but knowing he had to do something, toward the forward gun . . .

Under the tarpaulin, Boullard was talking, his voice low and harsh, all the kindly, old countryman's lines somehow vanished from the set, desperate face. "There will be a token resistance," he was saying to the men who were all sitting up, looking at the ground most of the time, looking up only occasionally at Boullard with a kind of deep embarrassment. "In a token resistance there are token deaths." He looked around him calmly from face to face, his thought plain in his eyes. "A token corpse feeds as many worms as any other. . . ."

Jouvet, the young one, was the only one who could not manage to sit still. He rubbed his heels back and forth making marks in the sand, and studying them intensely.

"Kill the pretty lieutenant," Boullard said, "and we have our own lives in our own hands. We dispose of them as we see fit."

"Let us look at it from the political angle," Labat said. "Politically, we are fried if the Germans win. . . ."

"Perhaps," Sergeant Fourier said uneasily, his voice full of the nagging pain of having to make a decision. "Perhaps we ought to wait and see what happens."

"We will wait and see ourselves buried," Boullard said.

"At least," said Labat, "we ought to talk to the lieutenant. Sound him out."

"I was on the Meuse," said Boullard. "I know better than to talk to a lieutenant. I'll take the responsibility. If you're all afraid . . ." He looked around him with savage, peasant contempt. "There're a lot of men still to be killed in this war. I don't mind making it one more or less, personally . . ."

"We have to talk to him first," Labat said stubbornly.

"Why?" Boullard asked loudly.

"Maybe he's with us. Maybe he wants to fight with the Americans, too. . . ."

Boullard laughed harshly. Then he spat. "I'm surrounded by children," he said. "If he's still an officer in the French Army after two years, he is not fond of the Americans. I am. At this moment, I am crazy about Americans. If there is any hope for anybody in this stinking year, it is in the Americans. I'm forty-four years old and I've fought in two wars. The third one, I want to pick my own side. . . ."

"Still," Labat said, his voice low and persistent, "still, we ought to talk to him."

"For myself," Corporal Millet said briskly, standing up, "I am on duty at the observa——"

He let his hands fall gently to his sides as Boullard brought his rifle up and touched his chest lightly with the bayonet.

"You are on duty here, Corporal," Boullard moved the bayonet tenderly on a breast button. "There is a question before the house that must be decided by a full membership."

Corporal Millet sat down carefully.

"I don't care," Labat was saying, grinning at Corporal Millet, "what you do to the fighting corporal, but nothing happens to the lieutenant until we talk to him." He patted Boullard's shoulder, in a small, reassuring gesture. Boullard slowly took his eyes off Millet and the corporal sighed.

Boullard looked around him searchingly at the men caught in this hour on this desert with him. Sergeant Fourier, haunted by dreams of a pension and his masseuse and still troubled by some obscure painful sense of patriotism and honor, refused to look at him. Jouvet, faced at the age of twenty with the ancient tangled threads of a bloody and complex century, looked ready to weep. Labat was smiling but stubborn. Corporal Millet was sweating and was making a great effort to look like a man who did not intend to rush to the nearest officer and announce a mutiny.

"All right," Boullard said wearily, "if that's what you want. Although I tell you, two words too many and we are all against a wall, looking at a firing squad."

Jouvet fumbled with his handkerchief quickly and Boullard looked at him curiously and impersonally.

"It is not necessary to commit ourselves," said Labat. His long, workman's arms waved in argument. "We approach the subject, we skirt it, we take soundings like a boat coming into a harbor . . ."

"Better!" Sergeant Fourier said loudly, happy at all deferment. "Excellent! Much better!"

Boullard stared at him coldly and Sergeant Fourier became quiet and nervously took out a pack of cigarettes.

"It's possible," Labat was saying, convincing Boullard, "to judge a man without a direct question. . . ."

"Possibly," Boullard said with no enthusiasm. "Possibly."

"I'll do the talking," Labat said. "I'm used to things like this. I have talked at union meetings for seven years and nothing could be more delicate . . ." He looked around him anxiously, hoping for a little laughter to take some of the deadly tension away, but only little Jouvet, who was always polite, smiled nervously because he realized Labat had meant it as a little joke.

"All right," Boullard said. He fingered his rifle gently and let it dip almost imperceptibly toward Corporal Millet. "I will judge. And you . . ." The rifle dipped very clearly toward Corporal Millet. "You will not open your mouth. Is that clear?"

Corporal Millet sat up stiffly at attention, feeling sorrowfully within him that his honor demanded some show of resistance and that his life would not be worth a great deal if he was incorporated in the army of the United States. He looked at Boullard's huge crushing hands, calm on the rifle. "It is your affair," he said faintly. "I wash my hands of it."

Boullard laughed.

Sergeant Fourier lighted his cigarette, gift of his plump wife the masseuse, eating her dinner comfortably, all unknowing, in the curtainy little apartment in Algiers with three exposures. He sighed and stood up and walked between Boullard and the limp Corporal Millet and stood at the edge of the tarpaulin in the full darkness, pulling with small comfort at his cigarette, while behind him, under the tarpaulin, there was no sound from the waiting men.

Lieutenant Dumestre made his way slowly across the rough black ground toward the gun position, turning over in his mind his possible opening sentences to the gun crew. "Men," he could say, "I am going to be absolutely honest with you. I am putting a white flag up beside this gun and I am delivering this battery over to . . ." Or he could say, "There is a possibility that tomorrow morning American troops will appear. Hold your fire until I give the word . . ." while silently swearing to himself that the word would never be given. There was much to be said for this method as it was indefinite and seemed less dangerous and didn't tip his hand until the last moment, when it would probably be too late for anyone to do anything about it. Of course there was always the possibility that he could stand up in front of the men and pour his heart out to them, remind them in ringing words of their country's shame, call upon them with blood and passion to forget themselves, forget their families in France, remember only honor and final victory . . . He could see himself, pale and fluent, in the dim light of the moon, roaring, whispering, his voice singing in the quiet night air, the men listening entranced, the tears starting down their cheeks . . . He shook himself, smiled wryly at the dream, remembering his harsh, slow way of speaking, plain, indefinite, without the power to move men to the nearest café, much less throw themselves grandly and thoughtlessly upon a doubtful and possibly fatal cause . . .

Oh, Lord, he thought, I am the wrong man for this, the wrong man, the wrong man . . .

He turned the corner of the tarpaulin, seeing the watchful, hateful shape of the gun outlined stubbornly against the starlit sky.

Sergeant Fourier was smoking pensively in the open and the other men were sitting, strangely quiet, under cover. When Sergeant Fourier saw him he started guiltily and threw his cigarette away as unostentatiously as possible. He stood at attention and saluted and with his right heel tried to douse the glowing speck in the dirt. Somehow, the sight of the small man with the comfortable little pot belly trying to pretend, like a vaudeville comedian that he hadn't been smoking, irritated Lieutenant Dumestre, who all morning and all afternoon had been grappling bitterly with war and fratricide and tragic, bloody policy . . .

He returned the Sergeant's salute curtly. "What's wrong with you?" he asked sharply, his high voice making all the men in the tarpaulin turn their heads coldly and automatically to watch him. "You know there's to be no smoking."

"Please, sir," Sergeant Fourier said stupidly, "I was not smoking."

"You were smoking," Lieutenant Dumestre said, weeping

inside because inside he knew how ridiculous this charge and countercharge was.

"I was not smoking, sir," Sergeant Fourier stood very straight and formal and stupid with the problem of the evening, almost happy to have a simple little idiotic argument to worry about at least for ten minutes . . .

"You've been told, you've been told!" Lieutenant Dumestre shrieked in his highest voice, mourning deep within himself for that womanly timbre, for his military insistence upon form and truth at this unmilitary hour, but somehow unable, with the Captain's departure and the imminence, potent and desperate, of the Americans over the horizon, to stop the high noise of his tongue. "At any moment we may be bombed. A cigarette glows like a lighthouse in a black desert at ten thousand feet! Why don't you draw a map of the gun position and publish it in the morning newspapers?" He saw Labat look at Boullard and shrug coldly and turn away with an air of dangerous significance and something within him clutched at his throat, but now there was no stopping that high, silly tongue, freed for a moment from the locked agony and doubt of the day's decision making. Here at least was familiar ground. Troops disobeying orders. Troops endangering security of the post or station. Troops slightly insubordinate, lying. . . . His weary, ragged mind, terribly grateful to be relieved of its unaccustomed task of painful exploration, relapsed into the formal, years-long grooves of Saint Cyr, of countless garrisons, countless lectures . . . "There will be double security tonight, two-hour watches for everyone," the voice still high, but with the three-thousand-year-old bite of military command. "An extra half day's ammunition will be drawn up from the battery dump by three this morning." He saw the men's faces bleakly collapse and also something else in them, although he couldn't tell in the rush of his commands what it was. Even as he spoke he hated himself for what he was doing, knowing that a better man would have ignored the cigarette or joked about it. . . . He hated Sergeant Fourier, standing there, pained and stupid and impassive, but in a way he was grateful to him, because he had given him the opportunity at this late hour once more for postponement.

He turned on his heel and strode away. Later, perhaps at midnight, he would come back, he told himself, and finally get this question of the Americans settled. He pulled his shoulders high in disgust as the sound of his own voice squalling about the cigarette sounded in his ears, but there was nothing to be done about it and he walked without looking back. Midnight, he thought, midnight is still time. . . .

Back under the tarpaulin, Boullard looked around him at the men. Their faces were grave, but except for Millet, there was consent in all of them.

Boullard walked out from under the tarpaulin with his rifle.

Midnight, Lieutenant Dumestre was thinking, when the bullet struck, midnight is still time. . . .

They buried him quickly without marking the grave and sat down in front of the gun to wait for the army of the Americans.

RETREAT

The column of trucks wound into the little square beside the Madeleine and stopped there, under the trees. They were furry with dust, the black cross almost indistinguishable even in the bright Paris sunlight under the harsh dry coat they had accumulated in the retreat from Normandy.

The engines stopped and suddenly the square was very quiet, the drivers and the soldiers relaxing on the trucks, the people at the little tables in the cafés staring without expression at the line of vehicles, bullet-scarred and fresh from war against the trees and Greek columns of the Madeleine.

A major at the head of the column slowly raised himself and got out of his car. He stood looking up at the Madeleine, a dusty, middle-aged figure, the uniform no longer smart, the lines of the body sagging and unmilitary. The major turned around and walked slowly toward the Café Bernard across the square, his face grimy and worn and expressionless, with the dust in heavy, theatrical lines in the creases of his face and where his goggles had been. He walked heavily, thoughtfully, past his trucks and his men, who watched him dispassionately and incuriously, as though they had known him for many years and there was nothing more to be learned from him. Some of the men got out of their trucks and lay down in the sunshine on the pavement and went to sleep, like corpses in a town where there has been a little fighting, just enough to produce several dead without doing much damage to the buildings.

The major walked over to the little sidewalk tables of the Café Bernard, looking at the drinkers there with the same long, cold, thoughtful stare with which he had surveyed the Madeleine. The drinkers stared back with the guarded, undramatic faces with which they had looked at the Germans for four years.

The major stopped in front of the table where Segal sat alone, the half-finished glass of beer in his hand. A little twist of a smile pulled momentarily at the German's mouth as he stood there, looking at Segal, small and pinned together with desperate neatness in his five-year-old suit, his shirt stitched and cross-stitched to hold it together, his bald head shining old and clean in the bright sun.

"Do you mind . . . ?" the major indicated the empty chair beside Segal with a slow, heavy movement of his hand.

Segal shrugged. "I don't mind," he said.

The major sat down, spread his legs out deliberately in front of him. "*Garçon,*" he said, "two beers."

They sat in silence and the major watched his men sleeping like corpses on the Paris pavement.

"For this drink," the major said, in French, "I wanted to sit with a civilian."

The waiter brought the beers and set them down on the table and put the saucers in the middle, between them. The major absently pulled the saucers in front of him.

"To your health," he said. He raised his glass. Segal lifted his and they drank.

The major drank thirstily, closing his eyes, almost finishing his glass before he put it down. He opened his eyes and licked the tiny scallop of froth from the beer off his upper lip, as he slowly turned his head, regarding the buildings around him. "A pretty city," he said. "A very pretty city. I had to have one last drink."

"You've been at the front?" Segal asked.

"Yes," said the major. "I have been at the front."

"And you are going back?"

"I am going back," the Major said, "and the front is going back." He grinned a little, sourly. "It is hard to say which precedes which. . . ." He finished his beer, then turned and stared at Segal. "Soon," he said, "the Americans will be here. How do you feel about that?"

Segal touched his face uncomfortably. "You don't really want a Parisian to answer a question like that," he said, "do you?"

"No." The major smiled. "I suppose not. Though, it's too bad the Americans had to meddle. However, it's too late to worry about that now." Under the warlike dust his face now was tired and quiet and intellectual, not good-looking, but studious and reasonable, the face of a man who read after business hours and occasionally went to concerts without being pushed into it by his wife. He waved to the waiter. "*Garçon*, two more beers." He turned to Segal. "You have no objections to drinking another beer with me?"

Segal looked across at the armored vehicles, the two hundred sprawling men, the heavy machine guns mounted and pointing toward the sky. He shrugged, his meaning cynical and clear.

"No," said the major. "I would not dream of using the German army to force Frenchmen to drink beer with me."

"Since the Germans occupied Paris," Segal said, "I haven't drunk with one or conducted a conversation with one. Four years. As an experience, perhaps, I should not miss it. And now is the time to try it. In a little while it will no longer be possible, will it?"

The major disregarded the jibe. He stared across at his command stretched wearily and incongruously in front of the Greek temple Paris had faithfully erected in her midst. He never seemed to be able to take his eyes off the armor and the men, as though there was a connection there, bitter and unsatisfactory and inescapable, that could never really be broken, even for a moment, in a café, over a glass of beer. "You're a Jew," he said quietly to Segal, "aren't you?"

The waiter came and put the two beers and the saucers on the table.

Segal put his hands into his lap, to hide the trembling and the terror in the joints of the elbows and knees and the despair in all the veins of the body that the word had given rise to in him, each time, every day, since the bright summer days of 1940. He sat in silence, licking his lips, automatically and hopelessly looking for exits and doorways, alleys and subway entrances.

The major lifted his glass. "To your health," he said. "Come on. Drink."

Segal wet his lips with the beer.

"Come on," the major said. "You can tell me the truth. If you don't talk, you know, it would be the easiest thing in the world to call over a sergeant and have him look at your papers. . . ."

"Yes," said Segal. "I'm a Jew."

"I knew it," said the major. "That's why I sat down." He stared at his men with the same look of bondage, devoid of affection, devoid of warmth or loyalty or hope. "There are several questions in my mind you can answer better than anyone."

"What are they?" Segal asked uneasily.

"No rush," said the major. "They'll wait for a minute." He peered curiously at Segal. "You know, it's forbidden for Jews to enter a café in France . . . ?"

"I know," said Segal.

"Also," said the major, "all Jews are instructed to wear the yellow star on their coats. . . ."

"Yes."

"You don't wear yours and I find you in a café in broad daylight."

"Yes."

"You're very brave." There was a little note of irony in the major's voice. "Is it worth it for a drink—to risk being deported?"

Segal shrugged. "It isn't for the drink," he said. "Maybe you won't understand, but I was born in Paris, I've lived all my life in the cafés, on the boulevards."

"What is your profession, Mr. . . . ? Mr. . . . ?"

"Segal."

"What do you do for a living?"

"I was a musician."

"Ah," there was an involuntary little tone of respect in the German's voice. "What instrument?"

"The saxophone," said Segal, "in a jazz orchestra."

The major grinned. "An amusing profession."

"I haven't played in four years," said Segal. "Anyway, I was getting too old for the saxophone and the Germans permitted me to make a graceful exit. But imagine, for a jazz musician, the cafés are his life, his studio, his club, his places to make love, his library and place of business. If I am not free to sit down on a *terrasse* and have a *vin blanc* in Paris, I might just as well go to a concentration camp. . . ."

"Every man," said the major, "to his own particular patriotism."

"I think," said Segal, starting to rise, "that perhaps I'd better go now. . . ."

"No. Sit down. I have a little time." The German stared once more at his men. "We will arrive in Germany a half hour later, if at all. It doesn't matter. Tell me something. Tell me about the French. We have not behaved badly in France. Yet, I feel they hate us. They hate us, most of them, almost as much as the Russians hate us. . . ."

"Yes," said Segal.

"Fantastic," said the major. "We have been most correct, within the bounds of military necessity."

"You believe that. It's wonderful, but you really believe it." Segal was beginning to forget where he was, whom he was talking to, the argument rising hot within him.

"Of course I believe it."

"And the Frenchmen who have been shot . . . ?"

"The army had nothing to do with it. The SS, the Gestapo . . ."

Segal shook his head. "How many times I have heard that!" he said. "And all the dead Jews, too."

"The army knew nothing about it," the major said stubbornly. "I, myself, have never lifted my hand, or done one bad thing against any Jew in Germany or Poland or here in France. At this point, it is necessary to judge accurately who did what . . ."

"Why is it necessary?" Segal asked.

"Let us face the facts." The major looked around him suddenly, lowered his voice. "It is very probable now that we are beaten . . ."

"It is probable," Segal smiled. "It is also probable that the sun will rise sometime about six o'clock tomorrow morning."

"A certain amount of revenge—what you call justice, will be demanded. The army has behaved in a civilized manner and that must not be forgotten."

Segal shrugged. "I do not recall seeing the Gestapo in Paris until after the German army came in. . . ."

"Ah, well," said the major, "you are not representative. You are a Jew, and naturally a little more bitter, although you seem to have done very well, I must say."

"I've done very well," said Segal. "I am still alive. It is true that my two brothers are no longer alive, and my sister is working in Poland, and my people have been wiped out of Europe, but I have done very well. I have been very clever." He took out his wallet and showed it to the major. The Star of David was tucked in so that it could be snapped out in a moment, and there was a needle already threaded, wound round a piece of yellow cardboard right next to it. "In a tight spot," said Segal, "I could always take out the star and put it on. It took six stitches, exactly." His hand trembled as he closed the wallet and put it away. "Four years, major, imagine four years praying each moment you will have thirty seconds somewhere to sew in six stitches before they ask to look at your papers. I've done very well. I've always found the thirty seconds. And do you know where I slept at night, because I was clever? In the woman's jail. So, when the Gestapo came to my house looking for me, I was comfortably locked in a cell among the whores and shoplifters. I could arrange that because my wife is Catholic and a nurse at the jail. Again, I've done very well. My wife decided finally she had had enough of me. I don't blame her, it's difficult for a woman. It's all right for a year, two years, but then the gesture wears out, you yearn not to have the millstone around your neck. So she decided to divorce me. A very simple procedure for a Christian. You merely go to court and say, 'My husband is a Jew,' and that's the end of it. We have three children, and I have not seen them for a year. Well enough. And the propaganda agencies, who also have no connection to the correct German army, also have done well. The French hate the Germans, but they have been fed the lies for four years and I think maybe they will never quite get over the lies about the Jews. The Germans have various accomplishments to their credit, and this is another one . . ."

"I think perhaps you're being too pessimistic," the major said. "People change. The world goes back to normal, people get tired of hatred and bloodshed."

"You're getting tired of hatred and bloodshed," said Segal. "I can understand that, after all this time."

"Myself," said the major, "I never wanted it. Look at me. Fundamentally, I'm not a soldier. Come to Germany after the war and I'll sell you a Citroen. I'm an automobile salesman, with a wife and three children, dressed in uniform."

"Maybe," said Segal. "Maybe . . . Now we will hear that from many people. Fundamentally, I am not a soldier, I am an automobile salesman, a musician, a pet-fancier, a stamp-collector, a Lutheran preacher, a schoolteacher, anything. . . . But in 1940 we did not hear that as you marched down the boulevards. There were no automobile salesmen then—only captains and sergeants, pilots, artillerists . . . Somehow, the uniform was not such an accident in 1940."

They sat silent. A passing automobile backfired twice, and

one of the sleeping soldiers screamed in his sleep, the noise echoing strangely in the sunny square. One of the other soldiers woke the sleeping man and explained to him what had happened and the sleeper sat up against a truck wheel, wiped his face nervously with his hand, went to sleep again, sitting up.

"Segal," said the major, "after this war is over, it will be necessary to salvage Europe. We will all have to live together on the same continent. At the basis of that, there must be forgiveness. I know it is impossible to forgive everyone, but there are the millions who never did anything. . . ."

"Like you?"

"Like me," said the German. "I was never a member of the Party. I lived a quiet middle-class existence with my wife and three children."

"I am getting very tired," Segal said, "of your wife and three children."

The major flushed under the dust. He put his hand heavily on Segal's wrist. "Remember," he said, "the Americans are not yet in Paris."

"Forgive me," said Segal. "I believed you when you told me I could talk freely."

The major took his hand off Segal's wrist. "I mean it," he said. "Go ahead. I have been thinking about these things for a long time, I might as well listen to you."

"I'm sorry," said Segal. "I have to go home and it's a long walk, to the other bank."

"If you have no objection," said the major, "I'll drive you there."

"Thank you," said Segal.

The major paid and they walked together across the square, in front of the men, who stared at them both with the same incurious, hostile expressions. They got into the major's car and started off. Segal couldn't help enjoying his first ride in an automobile in four years and smiled a little as they crossed the Seine, with the river blue and pleasant below them.

The major barely looked at where they were going. He sat back wearily, an aging man who had been pushed beyond the limits of his strength, his face worn and gentle now with exhaustion as they passed in front of the great statues that guard the Chambre des Députés. He took off his cap and the fresh wind blew his sparse hair in thin curls.

"I am ready to face the fact," he said, his voice soft and almost pleading, "that there is a price to be paid for what could be called our guilt. We have lost and so we are guilty."

Segal chuckled drily. By this time he was feeling exhilarated by the beer he had drunk, and the ride, and the sense of danger and victory that came with talking to the major in a town full of German troops.

"Perhaps," said the major, "even if we hadn't lost we would be guilty. Honestly, Mr. Segal, for the last two years I have thought that. In the beginning, a man is swept up. You have no idea of the pressure that is applied when a country like Germany goes to war, to make a man join in with a whole heart, to try to succeed in the profession of soldiering. But even so, it wasn't the older ones like me . . . It was the young ones, the fanatics, they were like a flood, and the rest of us were carried along. You've seen for yourself. . . ."

"I've seen the young ones myself," said Segal. "But also the older ones, sitting at the best restaurants, eating butter and steaks and white bread for four years, filling the theatres, wearing the pretty uniforms, signing orders to kill ten Frenchmen a day, twenty . . ."

"Weakness," said the major. "Self-indulgence. The human race is not composed of saints. Somewhere, forgiveness has to begin."

Segal leaned over and touched the driver on the shoulder. "Stop here, please," he said in German. "I have to get off."

"Do you live here?" the major asked.

"No. Five streets from here," said Segal. "But with all due respect, major, I prefer not showing a German, any German, where I live."

The major shrugged. "Stop here," he told the driver.

The car pulled over to the curb and stopped. Segal opened the door and got out.

The major held his hand. "Don't you think we've paid?" he asked harshly. "Have you seen Berlin, have you seen Hamburg, were you at Stalingrad, have you any idea what the battlefield looked like at Saint Lô, at Mortain, at Falaise? Have you any notion of what it's like to be on the road with the American air force over you all the time and Germans trying to get away in wagons, on foot, on bicycles, living in holes like animals, like cattle in slaughter pens in an abattoir? Isn't that paying, too?" His face worked convulsively under the dust and it seemed to Segal as though he might break into tears in a moment. "Yes," he said, "yes, we're guilty. Granted, we're guilty. Some of us are more guilty than the rest. What are we to do now? What can I do to wash my hands?"

Segal pulled his arm away. For a moment, helplessly, he felt like comforting this aging, wornout, decent-looking man, this automobile salesman, father of three children, this weary, frightened, retreating soldier, this wavering, hopeless target on the straight, long roads of France. Then he looked at the rigid face of the driver, sitting at attention in the front of the car, with his machine pistol, small, and clever, well-oiled and ready for death in the sling under the windshield.

"What can I do?" the major cried again, "to wash my hands?"

Segal sighed wearily, spoke without exultation or joy or bitterness, speaking not for himself, but for the first Jew brained on a Munich street long ago and the last American brought to earth that afternoon by a sniper's bullet outside Chartres, and for all the years and all the dead and all the agony in between. "You can cut your throat," he said, "and see if the blood will take the stain out."

The major sat up stiffly and his eyes were dangerous, cold with anger and defeat, and for a moment Segal felt he had gone too far, that after the four years' successful survival, he was going to die now, a week before the liberation of the city, and for the same moment, looking at the set, angry, beaten face, he did not care. He turned his back and walked deliberately toward his home, the space between his shoulder blades electric and attendant, waiting tightly for the bullet. He had walked ten steps, slowly, when he heard the major say something in German. He walked even more slowly, staring, stiff and dry-eyed, down the broad reaches of the Boulevard Raspail. He heard the motor of the car start up, and the slight wail of the tires as it wheeled around sharply, and he did not look back as the car started back toward the Seine and the Madeleine and the waiting troops sleeping like so many dead by their armored cars before the Madeleine, back along the open, unforgiven road to Germany.

PART IN A PLAY

Alexis Constantin was a pleasant man, and there were many people who thought he had talent, even before the war, when the theatre in Paris was crowded with good actors of his type, heavy, peasant-appearing men nearing middle age with an aptitude for shrewd comedy who could also be counted upon to be sympathetic and emotional when playing the aging rich husbands of flighty and unfaithful young women. He had been to Hollywood for a year or two and did an imitation of Boyer that was always amusing at parties. He had been married and amicably divorced when considerably younger and before the war had shared an apartment with Philippe Tournebroche, another actor, in the Saint Germain district. They had been friends ever since they had carried spears as young men together at the Odéon, and their friendship continued even though Tournebroche had become known as one of the most brilliant and successful actors in France before the Nazis came in and Constantin had merely plodded along, dependably, making a living, but always playing secondary parts, drawing a mildly approving paragraph from the reviewers here and there, but no more.

The actors' apartment was an agreeable place. Tournebroche made a great deal of money and was thoughtlessly open-handed with it. The two men got along together much better than either of them had got along with their wives, and there were a great many parties always going on there, with people from Broadway and Hollywood wandering through, and many bottles of champagne, and representatives of all the arts and always the new crop of pretty girls whom the two friends scrupulously shared, and a generous sprinkling of rich ladies and gentlemen with country places in Normandy and villas in Cannes who could be counted upon when Paris turned dull. All in all, it was the sweet, rich, glorious life it was possible for an artist to live in the 1930's and which we are repeatedly warned will never return to the face of the earth.

Occasionally, when he was offered a part in a new play, Constantin would have his bad moments. "The same thing," he said one morning to Philippe, morosely leafing through a new script. "Always the same thing."

"Let me guess," said Philippe. It was at breakfast, and Philippe was sitting across from him, meditatively tapping an egg. "An industrialist. You manufacture perfumes."

"Automobiles."

"Automobiles. A play of superior quality. Your wife deceives you with an Italian."

"A Hungarian. I have been cuckolded enough," Constantin said bitterly, "to have grounds for divorce against a nunnery full of English schoolgirls."

Philippe grinned. "Alexis Constantin," he chanted oratorically, "the eternal pillar of the French theatre. What would we do without the cuckold? The head reels at the thought. Pass the salt."

"Some day," Alexis said darkly, "they are going to be surprised. They're going to offer me this part and I'm not going to take it. This isn't a career—it's a disease. . . ."

"Some day," Philippe said gently, "you're going to play

Cyrano. I'm sure of it." Philippe was sensitive and decent and he was very fond of Alexis, and as much as he could do to assuage the pain of disappointed ambition, he did.

But these were only the occasional moments, the flashes of dark clarity when Alexis saw his career slipping hurriedly past in a confused, unremembered succession of drab roles. He was not jealous of Philippe, or as little jealous as an actor can be, and there was always the human dream that next year would be different, a last-minute change in casting, a friend dying in a difficult and rewarding role and he called upon to fill in between matinee and evening performance; a peculiarly discerning producer suddenly appearing on the Parisian scene and calling him, and saying, "Constantin, I've been watching you. You've been wasting yourself in those parts. I have here a new play in which the leading man runs from the age of nineteen to the age of eighty-five. He is irresistible to women and he is on the stage for two hours and twelve minutes. . . ."

But his friends never died, or died in bad roles; no discerning producers arrived in Paris; the pattern of his career was as even and predictable as wallpaper until the Germans entered Paris.

The Germans, who loved Paris much better than they loved Berlin, and who thought of themselves as connoisseurs and patrons of European art, interfered very little with the capital's theatre. Of course they closed down the plays written by Jews and handed Jewish-owned theatres over to more acceptable Frenchmen, for a price, and, naturally, they forbade the production of plays in which the English, Americans, or Russians were presented in a good light, but by and large they did no more harm to the theatre than a large motion-picture concern would do if given the same power.

The play Philippe was appearing in was a fiery story of the Franco-Prussian War, in which Frenchmen died eloquently on Uhlan lances in the third and fourth acts, so there was no question of its reopening. But Alexis was in one of his standard confections, acceptable to all parties except lovers of the theatre, and its producer was invited by the German commissar of culture, a romantic Bavarian colonel, to put the play back on the boards.

"It's a problem," Alexis was saying. He and Philippe had been talking around the subject all night. It was late now, and quiet outside, and there had been considerable brandy drunk over the problem.

"After all, I have only one profession. I am an actor."

"Yes," said Philippe. He was lying outstretched on the couch, staring into the brandy glass he held on his chest.

"A baker continues to bake. A doctor continues to practice medicine, Germans or no Germans. . . ."

"Yes," said Philippe.

"After all," Alexis said, "the play is one that was a success under the Third Republic."

"Yes," said Philippe. "That play was a success under Caligula."

"It does no one any harm."

"Yes," said Philippe. "Pass the brandy."

"There is nothing in it to give comfort to the Nazis."

"Yes," said Philippe.

There was a pause. From the street came the sound of marching, three or four men only, but the hobnails hit the pavement like an army.

"The Germans," said Philippe. "They march to weddings, assignations, toilets. . . ."

"Are you going to play this season?" Alexis asked.

Philippe rolled the liquor around in his glass. "I am not going to play this season," he said.

"What are you going to do?" Alexis asked.

"I'm going to drink brandy," said Philippe, "and read the collected works of Molière."

Alexis listened to the marching dying away in the direction of Montparnasse.

"Are you going to play next season?" he asked.

"No," said Philippe. "I am going to play the season the only Germans in Paris are dead Germans."

"You don't think it's right, even in a play like mine . . . ?"

Philippe waved his glass slowly past his nose. "Each man has to decide for himself. I am not going to influence anyone on a question like this."

"You don't think it's right?" Alexis persisted.

"I . . ." Philippe spoke slowly and softly into the large, delicate glass. "I think it's treason. I am not in the market as an entertainer for the brave, blond German troops."

The two friends remained in silence. From the street came a hoarse voice, bellowing a Schubert *lied*, and a woman's high giggle.

"Well," said Alexis finally, "I'll call Lamarque in the morning and tell him he has to find someone else for the part."

Philippe slowly put down his glass. He got up and came over to where Alexis was sitting. For the first time since the Germans had entered the city, Alexis saw emotion breaking through the bored, remote, cold mask of Philippe's famous face. With surprise, Alexis saw that Philippe was crying. Philippe held out his hand.

"I was afraid," he said. "I was afraid you wouldn't. . . . Forgive me, Alex, forgive me. . . ."

They shook hands, and Alexis was surprised again to see that he, too, had tears in his eyes as he clasped the hand of this man he had known for twenty years.

For a while it was not so bad. The Germans were correct, especially to well-known people in the theatre, and Alexis and Philippe remained aloof, pretending to be taking their time finding suitable parts, politely rejecting all manuscripts offered them. Philippe had a good deal of money, which he shared unstintingly with Alexis. They had a kind of prolonged vacation, reading, lying abed late, even spending seasons in the country after arming themselves with passes which were given graciously and without question by the Germans. There were long, quiet parties now at the apartment, at which painters showed new work which they refused to exhibit publicly, and playwrights read new plays that were meant for the boards sometime in the hazy future when the Germans were finally cleared out of Paris. That time, as the occupation wore on, seemed more and more dreamlike and impossible of achievement, and occasionally men and women of their circle would drop out and take once more their accustomed places on the stage, making their separate peace with the fact that the stalls were packed with German troops, in Paris on leave as a reward for their work on the various fronts.

The holiday began to pall on both Alexis and Philippe, especially as new faces appeared on the Parisian stage, new favorites claimed the attention of the public. Also, Philippe's money gave signs of running out and the Germans confiscated their apartment and they were forced to live, both of them together, in a small room on the fifth floor of a building without an elevator on a bad street in the Saint Denis section.

Finally, there was the day Lamarque sent a note to Alexis. He wanted to see Alexis alone and he wished Alexis to keep quiet about it for the time being.

Alexis dressed carefully for the interview, his best remaining suit, and a sober, expensive necktie he hadn't worn in two years. He had his hair cut on his way to Lamarque's office, and just before he went up the stairs bought a flower for his buttonhole. He mounted the stairs slowly, a solid, fleshy, handsome citizen, his face somber and reserved, hiding the sharp, nervous pangs of excitement and premonitory guilt as he opened the door of the producer's office.

"Germans or no Germans," Lamarque was saying, "this play"—he waved the manuscript excitedly above his desk—"this play is theatrical literature. It's a contribution to the culture of France. And the leading part . . . My God!" Lamarque looked religiously up to heaven. "An old man, but powerful, in the full flush of his maturity, on the stage half the first act, the whole second act, and a death scene in the third act Racine couldn't've done better." Lamarque was a little fat man from Marseilles with small, shrewd, dark, promoter's eyes. He had done well under the Third Republic, he had done well under the Germans, and he would do well under the Ninth Dictatorship of the Proletariat.

"Alexis," he gripped the actor's arm fiercely, "Alexis, when I read this I could only think of one man. You. I know the trash you've been playing. The same old thing, year after year. Same tricks, same notices. Death for an actor. This would be a new Constantin. Raimu, Bauer, they'll seem like schoolboys next to you. I've always felt that when the right part came along you could astonish the world."

"It's true," Alexis said tentatively, knowing that it was only because so many of the old standbys were no longer playing that Lamarque was talking to him, "I have somehow not had the opportunity to . . ."

"This is it, Alex," Lamarque said solemnly. "Believe me I've been in the theatre all my life and I know when a part and an actor get together like electricity."

"However," Alexis said, in a troubled voice, "it's very kind of you, but in a way, I thought I'd wait for awhile. . . ."

"He's a miser," Lamarque said reverently. "A huge, powerful miser. He's the hard-fisted, ruthless, scheming king of an industrial empire, with a pathologic love for money. He was disappointed in love in his youth and he has turned from women. All his passion is given to his money. His money is his wife, his mistress, his children, his life, and he ruins men with a laugh for a thousand francs. There's a scene when his best friend comes to him and pleads . . . but you have to read it for yourself, Alex, the power, the power, I don't want to spoil it for you. And there's a pure young girl he meets . . . And his change. The blossoming in December, the laughter. And then the discovery. The girl's a slut. Off with a captain in the Algerian cavalry at the moment he is buying a large pure diamond in a simple setting for her in the Place Vendôme. And a mad scene, Alex, a mad scene that makes *Hamlet* look like a game of dominoes on a Sunday afternoon. And the murder and the speech before he takes the poison! And the bloody, raging prayer to his God, with the glass in his hand! Alex," he said solemnly, "as God is my judge, this is the time for you to take your place in the history of the French theatre. . . .

Here!" He thrust the manuscript into Alexis' hand. "Don't say another word. Take it with you and read it, and come back to me at five o'clock this afternoon and take my hand and say, "Lamarque, I want to thank you from the bottom of my heart. I am ready for rehearsals tomorrow morning!"

A little dazedly, Alexis left the office. He walked slowly toward the Seine and sat down on one of the benches overlooking the river, and in the pale spring sunlight read the play. The play was written with bite and energy, and was not as lurid as Lamarque had described it, although it was studded with big, showy scenes for the principal character. As he stared unseeingly across the river, Alexis could imagine himself striding a richly lit stage, cruel, monstrous, pitiful, torn, charming, stricken, corrupt, murderous, suicidal, evil, calling down the powers of hell upon the world he was leaving behind him.

It was a role the vision of which had haunted his dreams ever since he had first set foot on a stage, and Alexis knew, as he walked slowly toward his apartment, that whatever Philippe would say, he was going to take it. . . .

It was a great success. Overnight his name became a tradition in the French theatre. The comic, aging cuckold was forgotten, and in his place was a tragic actor of historic stature. Every new script of any importance was submitted to him and he did two films in the suburbs that made his face famous throughout Europe. It was true that several of his more hotheaded friends cut him on the street and there were one or two savage articles about him in some of the flimsy resistance sheets that were unkindly sent to him and, of course, Philippe had broken with him, on that first afternoon. . . .

"Yes, yes," Philippe had said wearily, "I know all the arguments. Argument one: we must eat. Argument two: the baker bakes, the doctor medicines, etc. Argument three: the Germans have won and will continue to win. Are we to make no arrangements for the rest of our lives? Argument four: we all know French misers, must we only present Frenchmen as angels, etc? Argument five: I'm through with you."

And Philippe had packed and that was the last Alexis had seen of him. Later, he heard vaguely that Philippe was serving with the maquis in the Haute Savoie, and on one or two occasions had even been glimpsed in Paris, looking considerably older and shabbier than he had before. Alexis suffered a twinge of uneasiness each time he heard Philippe had been seen in Paris, but he was busy and successful and honored on all sides and consolation came easy.

It was in July, 1944, when Alexis next saw Philippe. The Americans were at Saint Lô, and Paris had become an uneasy city, tremors of guilt and joyful anticipation running through its secret life. Shots were heard in the streets at night, the Germans strode through the city searching the eyes of the inhabitants, calculating and puzzled; other Germans were found obscurely murdered along the river or floating face down toward the sea. Everyone knew that resistance battalions had been formed and the seventeen-year-old child who cleared the dishes from your table in a restaurant might be a Communist captain with an arsenal under his mattress and your name quite possibly on his list for retribution. Among the men who had done well under the Germans, or who had done nothing against them, there was a quiet, nervous, unhappy adding up of interior accounts. Alexis was no exception. He was not playing at the time and he took to long slow, speculative walks and sitting up late and alone at night, staring out the dark windows of his apartment at the waiting, trembling city around him. He followed the war maps closely, and examined his reactions as honestly as he could, and was pleased to see, that despite the danger to himself, he felt a thin, undeniable thrill of joy when the Americans broke through in Normandy and clearly took the road to Paris.

Philippe, when he saw him near the Etoile, was almost unrecognizable. He had grown much older, with gray hair and deep furrows in a face that had become very thin and weather-beaten. This, added to his clumsy clothes and heavy boots, made him seem like a farmer, and a poor one at that, committed to a bleak ten acres of unprofitable land, in town for a day. Alexis walked behind him, watching, and noticed painfully the harsh, wounded limp with which Philippe moved past the little tables of the cafés.

For a moment Alexis almost stopped, feeling that he must avoid this scarred, bitter-seeming veteran. But looking at the awkward, weathered, familiar back, thinking of the twenty years of friendship, twisted in the uncertain guilty currents of that bloody August, he walked more quickly, overtook Philippe, put his hand on his arm.

Philippe stopped, looked around. There was a quick, momentary tightening around his eyes, but that was all. "Yes, monsieur?" he asked politely.

"Please, Philippe," Alexis begged. "Don't say monsieur."

Philippe started to pull his arm away.

"Please talk to me. . . ." But Philippe began to walk away, deliberately, but not slowly, before the café tables.

Alexis followed him. "I'm sorry," he said. "I was a fool. I was weak. Anything you say. I should have gone with you. I've heard of what you've been doing. I'm proud you were once my friend."

Philippe limped slowly along, looking straight ahead, as though he heard not a word.

"Anything," Alexis said, pleadingly. "I'm ashamed of myself. I have a lot of money. I know you people need it. Take it. All of it."

For the first time a look of interest came into Philippe's face. He glanced sidelong at his friend, speculatively.

"Money buys guns," Alexis said hurriedly. "Everybody knows the Germans sell guns, but expensive . . . You haven't got the right to turn me away. No matter what you think of me. I want to do something to help. Maybe it's late, but I want to help. Myself, too. There'll be fighting. I'm willing to fight. Forget the last three years. At least, now, for the time being, forget . . ."

Philippe stopped. He stared coldly, without friendship at Alexis. "Don't talk so loud," he said.

"Forgive me," said Alexis humbly.

"And get out of here and go back to your home. And wait there."

"Will you come there?" Alexis asked happily.

"Maybe." Philippe shrugged, smiled sourly. "Maybe we will."

"My address is . . ."

"We know what your address is. Good-bye, monsieur." Without a smile, without a handshake, Philippe walked off. Alexis looked after the harsh, limping figure losing itself among the bright dresses, and the bicycles and the green uniforms in the sunlight, feeling sick for the lost twenty years, but also feeling a quickening and a hope he had not felt for months. He turned and went back to his apartment and sat there and waited.

"This gentleman," Philippe was saying, his voice touched with a light, scornful amusement, the first sign Alexis had seen of the long years this civilian soldier had spent on the stage, "this gentleman is known to me."

There were three of them who had come up to Alexis' apartment with Philippe just after dark. They were small, quiet men, very young, shabby and deadly-looking, and Alexis felt himself being weighed candidly and swiftly in their steady glances, as they sat across from him in his bright, comfortable living room.

"Early in the Occupation," Philippe went on, "he turned himself over to the service of the Germans, as so many did. . . ."

Alexis opened his mouth to protest, to say that continuing at his profession, keeping a theatre lit, in French, even though Germans did attend, was not so irrevocably sinful, especially when measured against the full-hearted co-operation so common in other and more important fields—but looking at the four, cool, quiet faces, he decided merely to sit there and remain silent.

"Now"—there was a slight stagey, amused mockery in Philippe's voice—"now the Americans are in Rennes and this gentleman has suffered a new growth of patriotism. . . ."

"Philippe," Alexis protested regretfully, "May I talk for myself?"

One of the other men nodded.

"I was wrong," Alexis said. "I wish to make up for it. Money. As much as I have. Myself, if I can be of assistance. It's as simple as that."

The three men looked at each other. Philippe turned his back, stared at a Derain drawing on the wall.

One of the men stood up, came over and shook Alexis' hand. The others smiled at him a little, with a touch of warmth, but Philippe didn't look at him, even when he took out the huge pile of franc notes and turned them over. Philippe did not say good night when he left.

When the fighting started in the city, at barricades and windows and on the roofs, they called for Alexis and he went with them, in old flannels, that he had used to lounge on the beach at Cannes, with the new armband that marked him as a member of the French Forces of the Interior. In the crowded room near the Hotel de Ville, waiting to receive what arms were available, with the preliminary crackling of automatic fire coming in through the windows, he looked again and again at the badge of acceptance on his arm. He felt too old for this and fear was a stone lump at the back of his throat and he was ashamed that his shirt was stained with nervous sweat, but when he looked down at the mark on his arm, there was a sense of religion and peace that almost compensated for the cold trembling nerves and the pumping blood.

They gave him four potato-masher grenades, which he stuck in his belt, after surreptitiously watching what the other men did with theirs, like a country cousin at a banquet watching the host pick up knives and forks.

Philippe came in and the room fell silent. Philippe stood before them and spoke in a low, even voice. "We do not intend to fight pitched battles at this point," he said. "We will harass them, pick them off when we can, try to make them stay and take cover and hole up until the Americans get here. We will try to make it expensive for them to move anywhere in Paris. We will be frugal with ammunition and weapons. I am sorry we are not better armed. Anyone who feels that he is not well enough equipped to go into this engagement is at liberty to leave. . . ." He looked thoughtfully at Alexis as he spoke. Alexis stroked the handle of one of the grenades.

Philippe came over and stood before him. "Monsieur," he said, "do you know how to use your weapon?"

"I—uh . . . Not exactly."

Philippe pulled one of the grenades out of Alexis' belt and showed him how to hold it, how to withdraw the pin, how to throw it. Alexis thanked him and Philippe gave him back the grenade and spoke sharply to all of them. "All right. We are ready. . . ."

They slid out into the night.

The next two days were a confused series of clanging dreams for Alexis; the first, biting smell of powder, the sharp, malicious chips of stone flying off window sills past your head and the mean, continuing searching noise of German machine guns, and a man falling beside you with a bullet through his lung and your taking his 1918 rifle and firing into the dust a hundred yards away and perhaps hitting the running gray figure there; and the heavy-footed trotting from one barricade of stones and tree trunks to another, with the inexorable noise of the Tiger tank turning the corner behind you and churning through the debris, and the hopeless, dissolving sound of shells hitting around you and the bloody disintegration before your eyes when the overturned car in front of you was hit by a shell and the two men and a woman pinned under it vanished . . . The boys around him were pleased with him and called him "Poppa" and loyally swore one of his grenades had fallen inside a tank turret when he dropped it from a third-floor window near the Opera and from time to time, in little flashes in the heat and fear and exhaustion, he was pleased with himself and surprised that there was so much of the soldier hidden under the boulevardier and artist. Philippe alone spoke to him coldly and professionally, not discriminating against him, but showing him no favor. Alexis did not mind. In the ambush and counter ambush, in the sudden burst from the roof, and the dry-mouthed stalking down the moonlit streets, there was no time to think of anything except the next German, the nearest cover, a hurried sip of wine to dissolve for an instant the stone of thirst and terror in the throat, a place to lie down and sleep for an hour to keep from dying of fatigue on your feet. . . .

He was alone with Philippe, hiding behind a wooden door that was just open a slit, so they could cover the street. Seven men of the group had just left them, going down the street to investigate the report that there were four or five Germans hiding in a wine merchant's cellar half a block away.

He could hear Philippe breathing hard beside him, because they had run a hundred yards down the broad street to get here, with two shots fired at them from snipers on the roofs. There were strange, wonderful colored gyrations of the atmosphere before his eyes and he heard his breath coming like the noise of some ancient machine, creaking and in need of oil. He sank to one knee, leaning against the door, feeling the door get wet from the sweat that was thick on his forehead. For a moment, looking up at the gaunt, red-eyed, scarred, be-stubbled face above him, wavering in the gyrating lights of his own exhaustion, he thought of Philippe and himself sitting across from each other, many years before at breakfast, the coffee steaming between them, the newspapers fresh and black before them, themselves newly washed in crisp silk robes. . . . "Your wife," Philippe had said jokingly at breakfast a long time ago, "deceives you with an Italian. . . ."

"They're going too slow. Too slow," Philippe was looking out the door. He had opened it wider and was watching his patrol cautiously make its way, hugging the sides of the buildings toward the wine merchant's cellar. "Stay here, he said to Alexis. "I've got to get them to move faster. . . ." He looked down at Alexis curiously. "Are you all right?" he asked.

With an effort, Alexis got to his feet, essayed a smile. "Sure," he said. "I'm a little old for this sort of thing. That's all."

"Yes," said Philippe and slipped out after the patrol.

He had only been gone five seconds when Alexis saw the truck. It ground around the corner and stopped for an instant at the end of the street. It was a big open German army truck, with a machine gun mounted on it above the driver's cab in front, and it seemed to be full of men, with rifles bristling on all sides.

Alexis threw open the door. "Philippe!" he screamed.

Philippe turned and he and the men of the patrol saw the truck just at the moment that the truck driver and the man at the machine gun saw them. The Frenchmen started to run and the driver threw his vehicle into gear and picked up speed, pursuing them. The machine gunner fired several bursts, but the jolting of the truck made him wild and the bullets ricocheted around Philippe and the others as they ran toward the corner, where they would get a moment's respite. Alexis took one last look at Philippe, the limping, exhausted figure running grotesquely, rifle in hand, with stone chips and machine-gun bullets flickering around him. . . .

Alexis left the protection of the doorway and began to run

across the street at an angle that would bring the truck even with him as it passed him. For a moment, no one in the truck saw him and he had time to pull the pin from a grenade as he ran heavily, diagonally, almost in the same direction as the careening truck, like a man running to swing on a trolley car. Then the machine gunner saw him and swung his weapon around at him. The first burst missed him and Alexis lumbered on, his breath singing weirdly in his ears, the grenade clutched tight in his sweating hand. The riflemen in the body of the truck saw him too, and the weapons appeared over the wooden sides, converging on him. Alexis never heard the shots, but he heard the sick whistle of the missiles past his head. One hit him high on the left shoulder and he stumbled, then picked himself up and, scrambling and stumbling, continued toward the approaching truck. The machine gunner swung his weapon around and there was the hysterical triphammer noise and Alexis felt something hit him in the head and there was the strange taste of blood in his mouth, although his tongue for some reason could not move to swallow it. He kept on, his shoes making a deliberate, shuffling, weary clatter on the pavement, amid all the other sounds, the grinding of the truck, the shots, the yelling German. His arms out to keep his balance, his legs moving with the insane deliberation of the mechanism of an automatic phonograph, staggering and sliding in his ruined fashionable flannels that had looked so well on the bright Mediterranean beach, blood streaming from his shoulder and head, leaving a plain dark wavering trail behind him on the pavement, his cheekbone exposed, broken and white in the bloody face, and the eye drooped close, its muscles torn and useless, and the other eye frantic and singed and dusty, he caught up with the rolling truck, put one hand on the cab, was dragged along for an instant while the man inside beat at the hand with the butt of his gun. With the homely, everyday grunt of a fat man swinging upon the platform of a suburban train, just reached in the morning, he pulled himself fcr a moment onto the running board and heaved the grenade up and over the wooden side into the mass of rifles and uniforms and ammunition and screaming men. . . .

He fell back and dropped peacefully to the pavement. Far off, it seemed to him, there was an explosion. Somehow he sat himself up in the middle of the street and regarded his handiwork with the one crazy eye. The truck had overturned and was burning brightly. Here and there a gray uniform dragged itself painfully for a yard or two, but most of the gray uniforms lay still and some were still burning.

The ghost and spectre of a grin crossed what was left of his face.

Philippe walked slowly up to him. Alexis brokenly raised one arm to wipe the blood and stone dust out of his one eye so that he could see his friend more clearly. For a single mangled moment Alexis thought of the things that lay between them, the thousand drinks and the pretty girls and the vacations and the idle debonair hours after the theatre and the afternoon he had been no more than an actor and had decided to play the big, ludicrous, sinful part . . . The bloody mouth and the broken teeth mumbled something, lost in blood, and the single wild eye stared up, dying, begging forgiveness.

But Philippe said, gently, but coldly, "Lie down, monsieur. We will look for the aid men."

Alexis shook his smashed, tangled head, grieving, knowing in this last instant that he was unforgiven, and lay down on the stained and fractured pavement.

THE PRIEST

The priest walked leisurely across the Besancon Bridge. The Doubs flowed swiftly past, springlike and ruffled and green, carrying with it a bright mountain breeze through the sunny valley. The priest was round and small and his dark, tanned face was rosy and cheerful in the pleasant morning as he walked with little steps next to the stone balustrade, keeping off to the side as a tank marked with the black cross rumbled past a wagonload of cabbages into town. Two young blond paratroopers, with their caps off, were leaning on the balustrade, staring quietly into the rushing water, their hair blowing in the wind, and the priest stopped next to them and stood by their side looking east to the mountains.

"Very pretty morning," the priest said, smiling.

"Excuse us, Father," one of the paratroopers said, haltingly, "we do not speak French. We speak only German."

The priest shrugged, smiled, patted one of the boys in a fatherly gesture, on the shoulder. "*Guten tag,*" he said, moving off.

"*Aufweidersehn,* Father," the boy said, standing up straight. He was almost a foot taller than the priest and he seemed very young, seventeen, eighteen perhaps, standing there with his hair blowing over his unlined, rather pale face.

The priest moved on, his small scuffed dusty shoes making a little mincing pattern under the swinging, worn folds of his cassock. He walked slowly along the busy street, pleased with the morning traffic, nodding agreeably at the housewives with their net shopping bags stuffed with vegetables. He stopped in front of one of the shops which was used as an art gallery, and looked at a local painter's water color of the Besancon cathedral, his dark round face grave with judgment.

In the same window, by the same artist, there were three plump, long-legged nudes lying in abandoned positions on rugs and sofas, and the priest glanced rather hastily at the pink and fleshy confections. A little grin played around the corners of his mouth as he turned away from the window and continued up the street.

He crossed the cobbled square at the end of the street, and, holding the skirts of his cassock, skipped nimbly and good-naturedly to dodge a large German army truck that was rumbling through. A little out of breath, and smiling, he walked to a table on the open terrace of the large café that stood under the new foliage of the trees along one side of the square. The man sitting at the table stood up as he approached.

"Good morning, Father," he said, holding a chair for the priest, and smiling with pleasure.

"Good morning, my son." The priest sat down, smiling at him, but sighing, too, as a fat man does at sudden changes of position.

The man seated himself beside the priest, so that they both could look out over the square and enjoy the fresh bustle of the spring morning. He was a large, slender man, with weary dark eyes and a sharp mouth and he was dressed in faded workman's clothes, with old, washed oil and grease stains evident here and there in the worn cloth.

"I hope," said the priest, "I didn't keep you waiting long."

"I just arrived," the man said.

The waiter trotted to their table. "Messieurs," he said.

"White wine for me," said the priest.

"Two," said the other man.

The waiter trotted off.

The man in workman's clothes surveyed the priest fondly, but with amusement. "Solomon," he said, "you're getting fatter every week."

The priest sighed. "Flesh is the curse of man. I live on cabbage and skimmed milk and I walk a hundred kilometers a week up and down mountain roads and I grow more and more like a pincushion. Still, Maurice, in a way, it has its points. Everyone expects a priest to be fat."

"That's true," said Maurice.

The waiter came back with the two glasses of white wine and the saucers. "Messieurs," he said, serving them. He trotted off.

The priest looked after him absently, noticing that there was no one at the near-by tables. "All right, Maurice," he said.

Maurice sipped his wine. "In Marcel Artois' barn, in the hayloft . . ."

"Yes," said the priest.

"On the road to Epinal."

"I know the house." The priest sipped his drink, nodding absently, his eyes squinted a little, looking out over the square.

"Two Sten guns with a thousand rounds of ammunition . . ."

"Well," said the priest.

"Three Enfield rifles with two hundred and fifty rounds of ammunition. A Luger and six grenades. How many men does Philip have with him?"

"Ten."

"Does that include you?"

"That includes me." The priest nodded.

"The difficulty with the child," Maurice said loudly, as two German lieutenants passed, "is that he refuses to recognize the authority of his mother."

"I will come by Wednesday afternoon," the priest said clearly, "and attempt to reason with him."

"There will be a gasoline convoy passing the crossroad two miles north of Epinal around eleven o'clock tomorrow night," said Maurice. "Ordinarily, the convoys are lightly guarded in this area, and there is brush right down to the roadside, and they stop at the crossroads for a minute or two to wait for stragglers. Tell Philip I suggest that that is the most profitable place. . . ."

"I'll tell him," said the priest.

"However, he understands," Maurice said, "that it is his business and I am merely offering suggestions."

"I'll tell him," said the priest.

"Messieurs?" The waiter was standing over them, questioning.

"Nothing more for me, thank you," said the priest.

Maurice put down the money for the drinks and the waiter cleared away the glasses and the saucers.

"Gasoline trucks," said Maurice, "make a very satisfactory target. They have a tendency to blow up."

"Philip will be pleased." The priest nodded again, with a trace of amusement in his dark eyes.

"Tell Philip I pray that God smiles upon your enterprise," said Maurice, very seriously.

The priest smiled a little. "I will pass on yours and God's good wishes. . . ."

Maurice turned and stared soberly at the priest for the first time. "Solomon," he said softly, "I think you are taking too much of a risk."

The priest grinned. "Again," he said, "the old song . . ."

"But to pretend to be a priest!" Maurice shook his head. "You're always on the verge of being discovered. Any curé with his eyes half-open . . . Any sudden or unexpected situation . . ."

The priest looked around him, his eyes crinkled. "I know this will offend your deep religious sensibilities, Maurice," he said, "but it is amazing how little people expect of the servants of the Church. And priests're always rambling around, poking their noses into other people's business. They make perfect messengers for the Underground. If we could really get the holy men of France into the movement, we would have a system of intelligence better than any telephone network. . . ."

"The Church has its own spiritual problems," Maurice said bleakly.

"Forgive me." The priest stretched out his hand and touched Maurice's arm. "I mean no offense."

"It still strikes me as dangerous," Maurice said.

The priest shook his head. "Look at me," he said.

Maurice stared at him. "Well?"

"In every magazine," the priest said, "on every wall, there are pictures of criminals against Germany who look just like me—Jews, swarthy, with thick lips, and hooked noses. . . . Why, Maurice," the priest said, grinning, "I could make a fortune as a photographer's model in Berlin."

Maurice chuckled. "I must admit . . ."

"But dressed like this . . ." The priest shrugged. "A priest is expected to look like anything at all in the world. Anyway, I've got away with it for three years now. I couldn't conduct Mass, but I tell my beads in public, and I carry a breviary and read a little Latin and I got a smattering of the sacraments from Father Morand before they killed him, and my papers look more authentic than a monastery full of Benedictine brothers, and the cassock is very handy when it comes to hiding my pistol."

Maurice stood up, smiling. "You always win this argument. Still, it gives me a chill every time I see you pass a church."

"I promise to defrock myself," the priest said, "ten minutes after the Germans're out of France."

"Well," said Maurice, "I must get back to work." They shook hands. "Good-bye, Father."

"I promise," Solomon said gravely, "to do nothing to disgrace the cloth. God be with you, my son."

Solomon sat at the table in the playful, sunny wind, watching Maurice cross the square. Maurice had a square, upright way of walking, and, knowing him, Solomon felt that by his walk Maurice betrayed himself to all the world—honest, righteous, devoid of subservience or fear. Each time, after their meetings, when they said good-bye, Solomon was moved by worriment and sorrow for his friend, and a bitter sense that they would not meet again. The trick was, in their business, to feel nothing, no affection, no sympathy, no regrets for the dead and dying. But fighting beside men in this obscure war, with your lives on the tips of each other's tongues a hundred times a day, with your life dependent every moment on their rectitude and sacrifice, you found yourself loving the good ones better than a wife or a son, and then the trick, of course, did not work. . . .

Maurice disappeared around a corner and Solomon sighed and stood up heavily, pulling his cassock down.

He stared back across the terrace, but at that moment a canvas-covered army truck drove up and the soldiers jumped out and the young lieutenant said loudly, "Nobody will move, if you please. All the patrons of this establishment will come with me, if you please. . . ."

Solomon looked at the corner to make sure that Maurice had disappeared and then sat down, sighing like a fat man, waiting for the Germans to reach him.

The interior of the truck was dark and crowded with some twenty patrons of the café. An odor of fear hung over the twenty heads and people attempted to remain frigid and remote from neighbors pressing on all sides.

"This is a formidable nuisance," one gentleman said in a loud voice, looking angrily at the impassive guard at the rear of the truck. "I have a very important business engagement at one o'clock. And I have a pass signed personally by General Meister, himself, who is a personal acquaintance of mine."

"I have a personal request," a voice cut into the semi-gloom under the canvas from near the front of the truck. "Please keep personally quiet."

"I will remember that voice," said the personal acquaintance of General Meister threateningly.

The priest wriggled a little on his bench and his two neighbors looked at him sourly.

"Excuse me," he said apologetically. "A fat man finds it difficult to be comfortable in his clothes. . . ." He put his hands under his cassock, through the side slits and pulled at his belt.

"What's the matter?" a man across the aisle muttered. "The priest wearing a corset?"

Two or three of the men tittered a little sourly.

"Excuse me, again," the priest said, lifting himself a little from the narrow wooden bench, under which there were some tow chains loosely stowed.

"Only the priests," said his neighbor loudly, "still remain uncomfortably fat in France."

Solomon sat back once more, sighing, a tiny smile on his lips in the darkness. Below him, hidden by the chains, lay the small pistol he had contrived to loosen from his belt and drop there.

"What did you have for dinner last night, Father?" his neighbor asked unpleasantly. "A whole stuffed duck?"

"God be with you, my son," Solomon said serenely, as the truck rattled into the courtyard of Gestapo headquarters.

Solomon was sleeping when they came to his cell and opened the door. It was near dawn and dark and cold and he woke shivering when the two SS men drew back the bolt and shone the beam of the electric lantern in his face, where he lay on the wooden bench that served the cell as a bed.

"You," one of the jailers said. "Get up."

Solomon sat up, rubbing the ruffled thin hair on the top of his head, still half-caught in the sharp darkness in the vague, delicious dream he'd been having in which he had been eating a large dinner in a warm, sunny café in Marseilles. A warm, peppery soup and lobster with a tomato sauce . . .

"Well," he said, blinking, struggling with the old, familiar cold knot of fear at the sight of the black uniforms, "well, gentlemen . . ."

"Get up."

Solomon stood up.

"Are you dressed?" The man with the lantern played it up and down the ragged cassock.

"Yes." Solomon swallowed and he felt himself shiver, thin waves of cold trembling from his groin upwards, finally tightening the skin on his forehead and around his ears in little spasms.

"This way," said the man with the flashlight.

Between the two SS men, Solomon walked out of the cell and down the stone corridor, his knees hurting as though the act of walking was a shocking and unnatural activity. Too bad, too bad, Solomon thought, licking the corner of his lips drily, as he followed the dark figure along the dim stone. He had thought that he was going to get away with it. His papers had been in perfect order, excellently forged, and they had searched him only perfunctorily and questioned him hardly at all, and had even been slightly apologetic, or as apologetic as you could ever expect a German to be. When he had dropped off to his cold sleep he had really thought they would release him in the morning. Well, he thought wryly, there are several different kinds of release.

The SS men stopped in front of a door.

"There's a man in there," the German with the lantern said, "who's going to be shot in a few minutes. He wants the last rites of the Church. Ordinarily, we are not so agreeable, but"—with a small grin in the weak light—"since we had the Church so handy this evening, we saw no harm in letting him make his soul comfortable. I, myself, am a Catholic, and I understand that a man, before he . . . At any rate, you have fifteen minutes."

He swung the door open and put his lantern down on the floor inside the cell. Solomon walked slowly in and stood still as the door closed behind him.

The lantern diffused a thin pale light along the floor, leaving the corners and walls of the cell in heavy darkness. A man was standing with his back to the door, his head lost in the shadows in the bare room. He turned when the sound of the Germans at the door had ceased.

"Father," he said softly, but mechanically, as though he had rehearsed the speech, "I am very glad you came. I have lived by the Church all my life and I believe in the life everlasting and I wish to make my peace with God in accordance with the sacraments before facing judgment . . ." The voice was bruised and muffled in the shadowy room, as though it came from a throat and lips that had been sorely torn and battered, but Solomon recognized it.

"We have fifteen minutes, my son," he said, trying to control the sorrow in his own throat. He stepped forward so that Maurice could see his face.

Maurice slowly lifted his eyes to look at Solomon. His lips were puffed and cut and three teeth were missing, with the blood still coming from the sockets. He held his hands stiffly in front of him. They were torn and swollen and covered with blood from the places at the fingertips where his nails had been torn out.

"The Germans told me," Maurice said evenly, "that I was lucky to be killed on just this night, being a good Catholic. They happened to have a priest here and they were releasing him in the morning. Shall we begin, Father?"

"Are you sure . . . " Solomon could not keep his voice from trembling.

"Yes, Father," said Maurice, staring at the door of the cell, behind which the Germans might or might not be listening.

Solomon sat on the small three-legged stool in the center of the room and, stiffly, with the pale light making his ruined face look clotted and grotesque, Maurice kneeled before him.

The jail was absolutely quiet and Solomon could hear the breath whistling brokenly through Maurice's smashed nose. Solomon closed his eyes, trying to remember some scraps of what Father Morand had taught him before the Germans killed him.

"Son, I will hear your confession now," he said, surprised at the clarity and steadiness of his own voice.

Maurice bowed his head at Solomon's knee. "Forgive me, Father," he said evenly, "for my sins. . . ." Then, in the quiet night, he confessed. He confessed to the sin of doubt, the sins of anger and murder, the sins of envy and desire, the sin of despair. Kneeling rigidly, his wounded hands resting for support on Solomon's knees, staining the old cloth with the slow dark blood, he spoke soberly and clearly, his voice swelling occasionally in the stone room, loud enough to be heard through the open grating of the oak door, if anyone were listening there. . . .

As the voice went on, Solomon remembered another man he had talked with, played another game with, before death. It was when he was a boy of fourteen and a neighbor was dying and too weak to leave the house and Solomon had gone every afternoon and played chess with the dying man in the sickroom. The man had once been fat and red of face, but now his skin was yellow and old and hung in loose folds from his bones. He was an avid player and loved to win, and occasionally cheated, moving pieces surreptitiously and taking back moves, falling back to his pillows in exhausted triumph after the game was over. Solomon had played with him on the day of his death, and at the funeral had watched with dry eyes as the coffin was lowered, the mourners and the cold earth, and stone crosses of the cemetery somehow mixed in his mind with bishops taking pawns and black wooden knights held in a yellow hand advancing over red squares. Ever since then, death and chess had lain in troubled confusion in his mind, funerals and ivory, flowers and squares, tears and pawns tumbled in a box mingling in obscure painful symbols in his brain. As he regarded his friend, kneeling before him, he felt as though he were betraying him in this double game of priest and chessman, and he wrenched at his will to focus all his pity and affection on the dying man. He put his hand out humbly and touched the bloody fingers of his friend. The Jews did it differently, he thought. They went into death hot and guilty, as to a roaring battle in a dark, bloody doubtful abyss, with intercession to their wrathy, fitful God not to be hoped for. He thought of the times he had seen Maurice coldly skirt death, and the times he had seen him wash his child's face, and of the times he had seen Maurice kill, with a rather abstracted, calm, regretful air, and of the times he had seen him walk side by side with his wife, dressed for Sunday, on the road to church.

As the voice went on in the cold stone room, Solomon thought of the times he had looked at Maurice's slender strained face, and known deep in his heart that he was going to die before their business came to an end. You felt that about yourself from time to time, and often about others, and you took a drink, or you got into an argument, and tried to forget it, but he had been sure of Maurice. Solomon was not a religious man, and he doubted that God would condemn Maurice because he had been shriven by a Jew, but he looked closely at Maurice to see if the orthodox Catholic soul, so obedient to the ordered sacraments and hierarchy, was suffering at the deception. But Maurice's face and voice were calm and clear, as though he were being granted absolution for all his earthly deeds by the Bishop of Rome, himself.

Finally, the droning broken voice stopped in the cold cell. Somewhere down the corridor there was the chilly clank of steel and a young German voice singing the mournful words of "Lili Marlene," the sorrowing, sentimental melody hanging cloyingly on the stale, condemned, frozen air. Solomon stared at the austere, destroyed face of his friend. If there were only some way of giving him one word to carry with him to the final wall, one word to tell him, you are loved, you will not be forgotten, we do not believe the shallow coffin and the quick lime pit are the end, we will mention your name later in the century . . . His hands groped in a small, lost gesture before him, but there was the sound of steps outside the door, and the fiddling with the lock.

He blindly ruffled the pages of his breviary and read a scrap of Latin for the absolution, and as the door swung open, made vague, wandering motions with his hands, from some dim memory of another deathbed.

Maurice stood up as the Germans came in. "I am very happy, Father," he said courteously as the Germans bound his hands, "that you were here tonight. I hope it has not interfered too much with your business in these parts."

Solomon stared at the Germans, knowing that Maurice was telling him he had not broken, that he had told the Germans nothing, that no plans were invalidated by his death.

"It has not interfered, son," he said. He stood up and followed them out to the corridor and watched Maurice walk away between the Germans, the familiar walk unchanged by the prison, or the cords on his wrist, or the knowledge that the wall was waiting. Maurice walked away, as he had walked away from the terrace of the café, the lean shoulders set square and upright, betraying himself to all the world.

A third guard came up to Solomon, touched his elbow. "This way, Father," he said, and led him back to his cell. He was sitting there, waiting for his deliverance, when he heard the small muffled sound, like a door closing sharply far away, from the other side of the prison.

NIGHT IN ALGIERS

It was late at night in Algiers and in the army newspaper office the clatter of typewriters had long since died down. Most of the men had gone to sleep upstairs and the halls were empty. The wisecracks and decisions and sudden laughter were over for the day, and in another building the presses were comfortably turning out the next day's paper.

On the walls, the pictures of all the pretty girls with big bosoms looked a little weary in the dim light. Down on the street outside the Red Cross building, late-traveling soldiers whistled for hitches in the dark and a soldier who had had some wine was singing the "Marseillaise" in English, the brave words and the brave tune floating up a little uncertainly through the darkness until a truck stopped and picked the singer up. In the office the radio was on and Tchaikovsky's piano concerto was coming in, moody and sorrowful, from London.

An assistant editor with sergeant's stripes on his sleeves came in and sat down wearily in front of the radio. He stared at it, remembering many things that had nothing to do with his job, remembering home and what his college campus looked like in June and how it had felt to sail out of New York harbor in the rain.

"Have some wine," said the reporter who was sitting there listening to the music. The reporter had no stripes on his sleeves at all. The assistant editor took the wine and forgot to drink, just sitting there holding the bottle.

"There's a bar in New York," the assistant editor said. "Ralph's. On Forty-fifth Street. Ugly little joint. I like to drink there. Ever been there?"

"Uhuh," the reporter said.

"Scotch whisky," the assistant editor said. "Cold beer."

The concerto ended in wild, mournful thunder and a polite English voice said it had been Toscanini conducting and Horowitz at the piano, the names sounding strange on the nighttime African coast. The polite voice said good night and the reporter got Berlin. There were waltzes on from Berlin, very prettily played, lilting through the small, paper-littered room. A polite German voice described the waltzes and once more the violins and trumpets swept out of the radio.

"The Germans," the assistant editor said. "They should be deprived of music for fifty years. Should be part of the peace treaty."

A rewrite man, a corporal, on his way up to bed, stuck his head in. "Anybody want a gumdrop?" He brought out the box. "Just got my rations today."

The assistant editor and the reporter reached out. They chewed consideringly on the gumdrops, listening to the waltz.

"Nice music," the rewrite man said.

"Fifty years," said the assistant editor.

The rewrite man yawned and stretched. "Going to bed," he said, and started out. "Maybe when I wake up tomorrow the war'll be over. Good night." He went out and the assistant editor washed down the rationed gumdrop with a little wine.

"Did you ever eat a gumdrop in civilian life?" he asked.

"No," said the reporter.

"Neither did I." He rolled the wine around reflectively in the bottle. "God, it's dull around here. I wish I could have gone to Italy." The radio turned to Hungarian dances and the assistant editor stared gloomily at it. He drank a little wine. "That's the trouble, though. Now that the invasion has come at last, other guys are covering it. Other guys'll write great stories. I'll be sitting here on my can in Africa. The editor. The assistant editor . . . When I got out of college I wrote better than I do now. Eight years ago." He rubbed his bald spot thoughtfully. "Somehow I got to be an editor. Eight years." He finished the wine. "Maybe I should've got married."

"Probably wouldn't make any difference," said the reporter, who was married.

"Probably not." The assistant editor shrugged. "There was a girl back in college in my sophomore year. She was a year older than me. You had to date her up in October for the spring prom. There was a fellow with a car who used to drive her to breakfast, lunch and dinner and send her flowers every day, but she used to take walks with me and lunch sometimes. She did the most marvelous thing that anyone ever did for me. I was a kid then and maybe it oughtn't to seem like so much to me now, but it still does. She broke a date with this other guy and went to the spring prom with me, I gave her orchids and we went to a couple of speakeasies and it was the best night I ever had in my whole life." He sat back, remembering the orchids and the speakeasies. "I introduced her to a friend of mine that summer. He had a lot of dough and called her long distance three times a week and six months later they got married. You can't blame a girl. Want to see her picture?"

"Yes," the reporter said.

The assistant editor took out the picture, yellowed and ravelled at the edges. It was of a pretty, graceful girl, in a white dress, sitting erect, a hint of strength in her face, mixed with ancient coquetry. "I don't know why I keep it," the assistant editor said, looking at the picture. "Maybe for luck." He put it back carefully into his wallet. He leaned back and his thick glasses and square, angular, plain, decent face shone in the dim light, clearly and painfully the face of a man who all his life might expect to find his best friends taking his girl.

"There was another girl. A Danish girl," the assistant editor went on. "I met her at a party in the Village. She'd come down from Boston with a friend, to be an actress. She worked at the Filmarte as an usher. I must have seen the last part of 'Grand Illusion' twelve times."

He smiled.

"I'd go around for the last reel or two of the pictures," he said, "and take her out to Sunnyside. She lived there with her friend. She liked me, but she wouldn't have anything much to do with me, even though I used to sleep out on the living-room couch five times a week. We had a fight and she decided she didn't want to be an actress and she went home to Boston. I guess I would've married her then if I hadn't fought with her so much." He took off his glasses and stared wearily at them. "About six months later she came down to New York on a visit and it was different. She moved right in and we had a wonderful time. We'd go out on weekends in the country. Just drive around in the summertime and stop in for drinks here and there and go swimming and laugh. She met me in Provincetown and we stayed with a Danish family. There was a great party. Provincetown, on Cape Cod. I don't think I've ever had a better time and I keep remembering it. . . . Maybe I should've married her. I don't know."

The assistant editor leaned over and put the bottle down. On the street below, three Frenchmen passed, singing loudly.

"I'm thirty years old and I write worse than I ever did. I don't know what I'll do after the war. Once, when I was in the Engineers, I sent her a letter. She was married, she wrote me, and she was having a kid on May seventeenth. She was going to call it David, after her husband's uncle, she said. She asked me to pray for it. I haven't written back. Well, what's the difference?" He put his glasses on again. "The Filmarte Theatre." He laughed and stood up. "I wish I had two hack writers I could throw stories to and know they'd come out right," he said. "I wouldn't get so tired. Well, it's pretty late. Got to go to bed. Tomorrow's another war."

The radio was sending out American jazz now, the deep, familiar horns of America pounding like all the music in all the dance halls and all the night clubs and at all the spring proms any American ever went to, any girl in a white dress ever danced at.

The assistant editor listened, his eyes blinking behind the thick lenses of his glasses. When it was over, he got up and walked into his own room slowly, his shirt dumpy and wrinkled, to take one last look at his desk and make sure everything was all right before going to bed.

MEDAL FROM JERUSALEM

"The question that haunts me," Schneider was saying in his high, soft voice, "is, my jazz, is it real jazz or is it merely European jazz?" He was leaning against the bar of the Patio restaurant between Tel Aviv and Jaffa, which used to be the old German consulate, and speaking to Lieutenant Mitchell Gunnison in short, gaspy bursts of talk, smiling a little sadly and a little archly at Mitchell, and occasionally touching his sleeve lightly with the tips of his fingers. "I mean," he said, "I know it's good enough for Palestine, but in America what would they say about a pianist like me?"

"Well," said Gunnison gravely, "I'd say they'd think it was real jazz." He was young and he spoke slowly and he seemed to think very hard before he answered a question.

"You don't know," Schneider said, sighing, "how you've encouraged me. I listen to the records, of course, but they're old, and you never know what actually is going on in America and, after all, we all know there *is* no other jazz, no place, and with a war like this, and God knows how long it's going to last, a musician gets out of touch. And once you are out of touch, you might as well die. Just die."

"You have nothing to worry about," Mitchell said. "You'll be a sensation in America."

"If I ever get there." Schneider smiled sadly and shrugged a little. "Anyway, you must come tomorrow. I'm working on a new arrangement with the drummer. A rhumba, Viennese style. It's ridiculous, but I think you'll like it."

"I'm sorry," Mitchell said. "I won't be here tomorrow."

"Then next night," said Schneider.

"I won't be here then, either," Mitchell said. "I'm going tomorrow. Leave's up."

There was a little silence and Schneider looked down at the bar and flicked his beer glass with his fingernail, making a frail musical sound in the dark oak barroom. "Some more fighting?" Schneider asked.

"A little more fighting." Mitchell nodded soberly.

"You fly, no doubt," said Schneider. "I have no wish to intrude on military information, but the wings on the chest . . ."

"I'm a navigator." Mitchell smiled at him.

"It must be an interesting profession. Measuring the distance between one star and another star." Schneider finished his beer slowly. "Well, *sholom aleichem* . . . That's good luck. Or, to be more exact, peace be with you."

"Thank you," Mitchell said.

"Hebrew," said Schneider. "I'm ashamed to talk Hebrew to anybody who knows it. The accent, they tell me, is frightful. But you don't mind, do you?"

"No," said Mitchell. He turned to the bartender. "Mr. Abrams," he said, "another beer please, for Mr. Schneider."

"No, no." Schneider waved his hands in protest. "The artist should not drink before the performance. After . . . Another matter . . . Ah," he said, bowing elaborately, "*Fraulein,* we are enchanted."

Mitchell turned around. Ruth was standing there, looking a little hurried and out of breath, but smiling and as pretty as ever in a light cotton dress, with her skin burned dark by the sun and her eyes full of welcome and pleasure at seeing him.

"I was afraid," she said, coming over to him and taking his hand, "I was afraid you were going to be angry and leave."

"I wasn't going to leave," Mitchell said. "Not until they closed the doors on me and threw me out."

"I am delighted." Ruth laughed and squeezed his arm. "I am so absolutely delighted."

"My presence," Schneider said, bowing, "I no longer consider necessary. A hundred thanks for the beer, Lieutenant. Now I must play or Mr. Abrams will start complaining he is not getting his money's worth out of me. Listen, carefully, if it is not too much of a bore, to my version of 'Stardust.' "

"We'll listen very carefully," Mitchell said.

Schneider went outside to the patio and a moment later preliminary erratic runs and fragments of melody came floating into the bar as he warmed up for the night's work.

"So." Ruth faced him, looking at him with an expression that was half ownership, half amusement. "So. What have we been doing all day?"

"Well," Mitchell started, "we . . ."

"You are the most beautiful lieutenant in the American army," Ruth said, grinning.

"Well, we went swimming," Mitchell said, pleased and embarrassed, pretending she'd said nothing. "And we hung around on the beach. And we flew a couple of barroom missions. Gin and grapefruit juice."

"Isn't Palestinian grapefruit wonderful?" Ruth asked loyally.

"Sensational," Mitchell said. "Nothing like it in America."

"You're such a liar." Ruth leaned over and kissed him lightly.

"There was an Eighth Air Force pilot down from England,"

Mitchell said, "and he told us how tough it was over Wilhelmshaven and we told the lies about Ploesti and then it was time to shave and come to see you."

"What did you think while you were shaving? Were you sad because you had to leave your interesting friends and see me?"

"Broken-hearted," Mitchell said.

"You've got such a nice, skinny face," Ruth touched the line of his jaw. "You're as pretty as an English lieutenant. I'm not fond of the English, but they have the prettiest lieutenants of any army."

"We send our pretty ones to the Pacific," said Mitchell. "Guadalcanal. We preserve them for American womanhood."

Ruth signaled Mr. Abrams for a drink. "I was in Jerusalem today. I told my boss I was sick and went there. It's so bad—we never got to see Jerusalem together."

"Some other time," Mitchell said. "I'll come back and we'll see Jerusalem."

"Don't lie to me," Ruth said, seriously. "Please don't lie. You won't come back. You won't see me again. Absolutely no lies, please."

Mitchell felt very young. He felt there was something to be said, and an older man would know how to say it, but he felt dumb and bereaved and clumsy and it must have showed on his face as he peered at his glass, because Ruth laughed and touched his lips with her fingers and said, "You have such a tragic face for an American. Where do you come from in America?"

"Vermont," Mitchell said.

"Has everybody got a face like yours in Vermont?"

"Everybody."

"I will visit there," Ruth drained her glass, "at some later date."

"I'll give you my address," Mitchell said.

"Of course," said Ruth politely. "You must write it down some time."

They went out into the patio and sat down at a table on the old flagstones under a palm tree, with the blue blackout lights shining dimly over the uniforms and pale dresses, and the moon riding over the Mediterranean and casting flickering shadows over the dancers who now claimed the spot where the German consul had lived well in days gone by. Mitchell ordered champagne because it was his last night. It was Syrian champagne, but not bad, and to both of them it gave an air of festivity and importance to the evening, as it rocked in its silver bucket of ice. Eric, the waiter with the limp, ceremoniously took Ruth's ration tickets, and Schneider, seated with the drummer across the patio, with the drum dimly lit from inside by an orange light of which Schneider was very proud, played "Summertime" because he had decided that was the song Mitchell liked best. The old song, played trickily and well in the soft, echoing patio somehow sounded, by some ineradicable stamp in Schneider's blood, like Carolina and Vienna and the Balkans, with here and there chords of an old Hebrew chant, quite just and indigenous here between the heavy stone walls on the edge of the Sinai desert.

"I'm jealous of him," said Ruth, speaking over the edge of her glass.

"Who?"

"Schneider."

"Why?" Mitchell asked.

"Because of the way he looks at you. He's crazy about you. Has he asked you to come to tea with him and his mother?"

"Yes," said Mitchell, trying not to smile.

"I'll tear his eyes out," Ruth said. "I'm jealous of anybody who looks at you that way. The girls back in Vermont and those Red Cross girls."

"You have nothing to worry about," Mitchell said. "Nobody looks at me that way. Not even Schneider or you."

"That's the nicest thing about you," Ruth said. "You don't know anything. I'm so used to men who know just how many steps out of bed each look a woman gives them measures. I must visit America after the war. . . ."

"Where will you really go?" Mitchell asked. "Back to Berlin?"

"No." Ruth stared reflectively down at her plate. "No, not back to Berlin. Never back to Berlin. The Germans have made clear their feeling about me. A little thing like a war will not change them. The lamb does not go back to the slaughter house. Anyway, I have nobody there. There was a young man . . ." She leaned over and picked up the bottle and absently poured for Mitchell and herself. "I don't know what happened to him. Stalingrad, maybe, Alamein . . . Who knows?"

Four men came into the patio and walked through the brief illumination of the blue lights. Three of them were Arabs in European dress, and the fourth was a man in the uniform of the American army with the civilian technical adviser patch on his shoulder. They stopped at the table. The three Arabs bowed a little, ceremoniously, to Ruth, and the American said, "I thought you were sick."

"This is Mr. Carver," Ruth said to Mitchell, with a wave to the American. "He's my boss."

"Hi, Lieutenant," said Carver. He was a big, fat man, with a weary, puffy, intelligent face. He turned back to Ruth. "I thought you were sick," he repeated in a pleasant, loud, slightly drunken voice.

"I was sick," Ruth said, cheerfully. "I had a miraculous recovery."

"The American army," Carver said, "expects every civilian worker to do her duty."

"Tomorrow," said Ruth. "Now please go away with your friends. The lieutenant and I are having an intimate talk."

"Lieutenant . . ." It was one of the Arabs, the shortest of the three, a slight, dark man, with a round face and liquid, veiled eyes. "My name is Ali Khazen. Permit me to introduce myself, as no one here seems to remember his manners well enough to do so."

Mitchell stood up. "Mitchell Gunnison," he said, putting out his hand.

"Forgive me," Carver said. "I'm suffering from drink. This is Sayed Taif . . ." He indicated the tallest of the Arabs, a middle-aged man with a severe, handsome, tight-lipped face. Mitchell shook hands with him.

"He doesn't like Americans," Carver said loudly. "He's the leading journalist of the local Arab world and he writes for thirty-five papers in the United States and he doesn't like Americans."

"What was that?" Taif asked politely, inclining his head in a reserved, small gesture.

"Also, he's deaf," said Carver. "Most useful equipment for any journalist."

Nobody bothered to introduce the third Arab who stood a little to one side, watching Taif with a fierce, admiring stare, like a boxer dog at his master's feet.

"Why don't you all go away and eat your dinner?" Ruth said.

"Lieutenant," Carver said, ignoring her, "take the advice of a veteran of the Middle East. Do not become involved with Palestine."

"He's not becoming involved with Palestine," Ruth said. "He's becoming involved with me."

"Beware Palestine." Carver weaved a little as he spoke. "The human race is doomed in Palestine. For thousands of years. They chop down the forests, burn down the cities, wipe out the inhabitants. This is no place for an American."

"You drink too much, Mr. Carver," Ruth said.

"Nevertheless," Carver shook his big head heavily. "It is no accident that they picked this place to crucify Christ. You couldn't pick a better place to crucify Christ if you scoured the maps of the world for five hundred years. I'm a Quaker myself, from the city of Philadelphia, Pennsylvania, and all I see here is the blood of bleeding humanity. When this war is over I'm going back to Philadelphia and wait until I pick up the morning newspaper and read that everybody in Palestine has exterminated everybody else in Palestine the night before." He walked unsteadily over to Ruth's chair and bent over and peered intently into her face. "Beautiful girl," he said, "beautiful, forlorn girl." He straightened up. "Gunnison, I admonish you, as an officer and gentleman, do not harm one hair on this beautiful girl's head."

"Every hair," Mitchell said, gravely, "is safe with me."

"If you must drink," Ruth said to Carver sharply, "why don't you do it with Americans? Why do you have to go around with bandits and murderers like these?" She waved her hand toward the Arabs. The journalist smiled, his handsome face frosty and amused in the wavering light.

"Impartiality," Carver boomed. "American impartiality. We

are famous for it. We are nobody's friend and nobody's enemy. We merely build airfields and pipelines. Impartially. Tomorrow I lunch with the President of the Jewish Agency."

Ruth turned to the journalist. "Taif," she said, loudly. "I read your last piece."

"Ah, yes," he said, his voice a little dead and without timbre. "Did you like it?"

"You'll be responsible for the death of thousands of Jews," said Ruth.

"Ah, thank you," he said. He smiled. "It is my fondest hope." He turned to Mitchell. "Naturally, Lieutenant," he said, "our charming little Ruth is biased in the matter. It is necessary to give the Arab side of the proposition." He began to speak more seriously, with a severe, oratorical emphasis, like an evangelical preacher. "The world is dazzled by the Jewish accomplishment in Palestine. Fine, clean cities, with plumbing. Industries. Where once was desert, now the rose and the olive bloom. Et cetera."

"Taif, old boy," Carver pulled at his arm, "let's eat and you can lecture the lieutenant some other time."

"No, if you please." The journalist pulled his arm politely away from Carver's hand. "I welcome the opportunity to talk to our American friends. You see, my good Lieutenant, you may be very pleased with the factory and the plumbing, and perhaps, even, from one point of view, they may be good things. But they have nothing to do with the Arab. Perhaps the Arab prefers the desert as it was. The Arab has his own culture . . ."

"When I hear the word 'culture'," Carver said, "I reach for my pistol. What famous American said that?"

"To Americans and Europeans," the journalist went on, in

his singsong, dead voice, "the culture of the Arab perhaps seems backward and dreadful. But, forgive us, the Arab prefers it. The virtues which are particularly Arab are kept alive by primitive living. They die among the plumbing."

"Now," said Ruth, "we have heard a new one. Kill the Jew because he brings the shower bath."

The journalist smiled indulgently at Ruth, as at a clever child. "Personally," he said, "I have nothing against the Jews. I swear that I do not wish to harm a single Jew living in Palestine today. But I will fight to the death to keep even one more Jew from entering the country. This is an Arab state, and it must remain an Arab state."

"Gunnison," Carver said, "aren't you glad you came?"

"Six million Jews have died in Europe," Ruth said, her voice harsh and passionate and surprising to Mitchell. "Where do you want the survivors to go?" She and the journalist had forgotten the rest of them and were locked with each other across the table.

The journalist shrugged and looked for a moment up above the palm fronds at the dark sky. "That," he said, "is a question for the world to decide. Why must the poor Arab have the whole decision? We've taken in much more than our share. If the rest of the world really wants to see the Jewish race survive let them take them in. America, Britain, Russia . . . I do not notice those large countries taking in great masses of Jews."

"There are no great masses," Ruth said. "There is only a handful."

Taif shrugged. "Even so. The truth may be, perhaps," he paused, a little doubtfully, reminding Mitchell of an old Latin teacher in a class in Cicero, shrewdly hesitating for effect, before telling the class whether the word in question was in the ablative or dative absolute, "the truth may be that the rest of the world really wants to see the Jewish race die out." He turned and smiled warmly at Mitchell. "It is an interesting supposition, Lieutenant. It might be most interesting to examine it before talking any more about Palestine." He walked over to Ruth and leaned over and kissed her fleetingly on the forehead. "Good night, little Ruth," he said, and went to a table across the patio, with the silent, adoring Arab behind him.

"If I see you with that man once more," Ruth spoke to the man who had introduced himself to Mitchell, and who had remained standing at their table, "I'll never talk to you again."

The Arab looked swiftly at Mitchell, a veiled, probing flick of the eyes, and said something to Ruth in Arabic.

"No," said Ruth, her voice clipped and sharp. "Definitely no."

The Arab bowed slightly, put out his hand to Mitchell and, as they shook hands, said, "Very pleasant meeting you, Lieutenant," and went off to join his friends at their table.

"Thé dansants in old Tel Aviv," said Carver. "Bring the kiddies. Good night." He waddled over to the other table.

"Ruth," Mitchell started to talk.

"Lieutenant Gunnison . . ." It was the soft, apologetic voice of Schneider at his elbow. "I am so anxious for your opinion. What did you think of 'Stardust'?"

Mitchell turned slowly from staring at Ruth, who was sitting tense and upright in her chair. "Great, Schneider," Mitchell said. "I thought it was sensational."

Schneider beamed with pleasure. "You are too kind," he said. "I will play you 'Summertime' once more."

"Thanks a lot," said Mitchell. He put out his hand and covered Ruth's, lying on the table. "You all right?" he asked.

She smiled up at him. "Sure," she said. "I am an admirer of abstract political discussions." Her face grew serious. "Do you want to know what Khazen asked when he spoke to me in Arabic?"

"Not if you don't want to tell me."

"I want to tell you." Ruth absently caressed his fingers. "He asked me if I would meet him later."

"Yes," said Mitchell.

"I told him no."

"I heard you." Mitchell grinned at her. "They probably heard you in Cairo."

"I didn't want you to feel disturbed or doubtful," Ruth said, "your last night."

"I feel fine," Mitchell said.

"I've been going with him for four years." She played for a moment with the food on the plate that the waiter had put before her. "When I came here in the beginning I was frightened and lonely and he was very decent. He's a contractor for the Americans and British and he's made a fortune during the war. But when Rommel was outside Alexandria he and his friends used to celebrate in secret. I can't stand him any more. I tell him when I take up with other men. But he hangs on. Ah, finally, I suppose he'll get me to marry him. I'm not strong enough any more." She looked up at Mitchell and tried to smile. "Don't be shocked, darling," she said. "Americans can't understand how tired the human race can get." She stood up suddenly. "Let's dance."

They went onto the floor and Schneider broke into "Summertime" when he saw them and smiled fondly at them as they danced. She danced very well, lightly and passionately, and Mitchell knew as he danced that he was going to remember this for a long time, at odd moments, swinging away from targets with the flak falling off behind him, and later, if he made it, in the snowy hills of his home state, the light, soft pressure of the bright cotton dress, the dark, curved, delicate face below his, the hushed sound of their feet on the old floor under the palms, the clever rich music of the piano under the small blue lights strung out from the stone building. There were a million things that crowded his throat that he wanted to tell her, and there was no way of saying them. He kissed her cheek as the music ended and she glanced up at him, and smiled and said, "There, that's better," and they were laughing by the time they got back to their table.

He paid the bill and they went out, saying good night to Schneider, not looking back at the table where Carver and the three Arabs sat, but hearing Carver's deep voice rolling through the music and the darkness, calling, "Does any one want an airfield? I'll build it for him. Does anyone want a crown of thorns? I'll build it for him."

There was an old carriage waiting outside the restaurant, its driver dozing and its lights dimmed and they climbed in and sat close together as the driver clucked to the horse and they rattled slowly back toward town. The breeze had gone down as it did at nine o'clock every night and there was a small warm breath of salt off the Mediterranean and every once in awhile a jeep rushed past in a whistle of American wind, with its slits of cat's-eye lights cutting a darting, frail skidding pattern in the darkness, making the creakings and rustlings of the old carriage older and dearer and more private as they sat there holding on to each other in silence.

They got off a block from where Ruth lived because the people from whom she rented her room were intensely moral and did not approve of their border going out with soldiers. They walked past the corner where the Italian bombers had killed a hundred and thirty people on a Friday morning the year before and turned into Ruth's street. From a darkened window came the sound of someone practising the third movement of the Brahms' violin concerto and Mitchell couldn't help smiling and realizing that one of his strongest memories of Tel Aviv would be the strains of Tschaikovsky and Brahms and Beethoven coming through the opened windows on every street of the town, as the furiously cultured inhabitants practiced runs and cadenzas with never-ending zeal.

All the houses were blacked out, but there was a tiny sliver of light along one of the windows in the third-floor apartment in which Ruth lived and they stopped in dismay when they saw it.

"She's up," Ruth said.

"Doesn't she ever sleep?" Mitchell asked angrily.

Ruth giggled and kissed him. "She can't stay up forever," Ruth said. "We'll take a little walk and by the time we get back she'll be asleep."

Mitchell took her arm and they walked slowly down toward the sea. Soldiers and whores and fat, placid couples strolled on the concrete walk along the beach and the Mediterranean heaved gently under the moon and broke in small white rolls of foam against the beach, with a steady, foreign grumble, not like the roar of the Atlantic on the cold northern beaches of home. From a café a hundred yards away came the sound of a string quartet playing a Strauss waltz as though Vienna had never been taken, the waltz never lost to the enemy.

Mitchell and Ruth went down the steps to the beach. A weaving British lance-corporal coming up the steps with a girl, stiffened and saluted rigidly, his hand quivering with respect for authority and Mitchell saluted back, and Ruth giggled.

"What're you laughing at?" Mitchell asked, when they had passed the lance-corporal.

"I laugh," Ruth said, "every time I see you salute."

"Why?"

"I don't know why. I just laugh. Forgive me." She took off her shoes and walked barefoot in the sand up to the water's edge. The sea swept softly in from Gibraltar and Tunis and Cyrene and Alexandria and lapped at her toes.

"The Mediterranean," Ruth said. "I hate the Mediterranean."

"What's the matter with it?" Mitchell stared out at the flickering silver path of the moon over the water.

"I was on it," Ruth said, "for thirty-three days. In the hold of a Greek steamer that used to carry cement. Maybe I oughtn't to tell you things like that. You're a tired boy who's been sent here to have a good time so he can go back and fight well. . . ."

"You tell me anything you want to tell me," Mitchell said. "I'll fight all right."

"Should I tell you about Berlin, too? Do you want to hear about Berlin?" Ruth's voice was hard and cold, and somehow a little sardonic, not at all like her voice as he had heard it in the whole week he had known her. The meeting with the journalist at the restaurant had started something stirring within her, something that he hadn't seen before, and he felt that before he left he should see that side of her too.

"Tell me about Berlin," Mitchell said.

"I worked for a newspaper," Ruth said, her toes digging lightly in the sand, "even after the Nazis came in, and I was in love with the man who wrote the Economics column and he was in love with me. . . ."

"Economics?" Mitchell was puzzled.

"The stock exchange. The prophecies and excuses."

"Oh," said Mitchell, trying to picture what a man who wrote stock-exchange tips in Berlin in 1934 would look like.

"He was very gay," Ruth said. "Very young, but elegant, with checkered vests and he wore a monocle and he lost all his money at the races. His name was Joachim. He used to take me to the races and to the cafés and it used to drive my mother crazy, because if they ever found out I was a Jewish girl out with a Gentile man, they would have sentenced me to death for polluting the bloodstream of the German nation. They'd have sent him to a concentration camp, too, but he was always easy and laughing, and he said, 'The important thing is to be brave,' and we were never questioned and I went to every night club in Berlin, even nights that Goering and Goebbels were in the same room.

"My father was taken to a concentration camp and we decided it was time for me to leave and Joachim got together all the money he could lay his hands on and gave it to me and I went to Vienna. I was supposed to go to Palestine, if I could, and send for my mother, and for my father, too, if he ever got out of the concentration camp. There was an office in Vienna, and it was filled with refugees from all over Germany, and we collected money to buy transportation and bribe the nations of the world to let some of us in. I slept in the bathtub and talked to sailors and thieves and murderers and crooked shipowners and finally we got a Greek steamer that was supposed to put in at Genoa and pick us up if we managed to get there. We gave the man 75,000 dollars in cash in advance because that's the only way he would do it, and somehow we got the Austrian government and the Italian government to look the other way, at a price, and they piled us into freight cars, eight hundred of us, and locked us in, men, women and children, lying one on top of another, and the trip took a week and a day to Genoa and when we got there the ship never arrived. The Greek took the 75,000 dollars and disappeared. There are all kinds of Greeks, and I have nothing against them, but this was a bad one. Then the Italian government sent us back to Vienna and six people committed suicide because they couldn't bear it, and we started in all over again."

Mitchell stared out at the dark line of the sea where it blended in the western distance with the purple of the sky. He tried to think of what it would have been like for his sister and mother if they had been locked into freight cars at Rutland and forced to travel for eight days up to Quebec, say, to wait for an illegal ship to an unknown country. His mother was tall and white-haired and unruffled and pleasant, and his sister was cool and pretty and had some irritating superior mannerisms that she had picked up when she had been foolishly sent for a year to a fancy girls' finishing school in Maryland.

"Let's start home," Ruth said. "If my landlady's still up, we'll shoot her."

They turned their backs on the quiet white churn of the waves and walked, hand in hand, across the heavy sand of the beach toward the black pile of the buildings of the city.

"Well," Mitchell said, "I want to hear the rest of it."

"No, you don't," Ruth said. "Forgive me for telling you so much. It's too dreary."

"I want to hear," Mitchell said. In the week he had known Ruth, she had been gay and light-hearted and had helped him to forget the planes spinning out of control and the dying men lying in their frozen blood on the tangled wires and broken aluminum of the Liberator floors, and now he felt as though he owed it to himself and to Ruth to take back with him some of her agony, too, not only the laughter and the tender jokes and the self-effacing merriment. Suddenly, tonight, she had become terribly dear to him, and he felt responsible to her in a way he had never felt responsible to a girl before.

"Tell me," he said.

Ruth shrugged. "Back in Vienna," she said, "we did it all over again. It took two months and the police caught a lot of us and it meant hiding and running most of the time, but we collected the money again, and we found ourselves another Greek, and this time he turned out to be honest. Or at least as honest as people were to Jews without passports in those days in Europe. We got down to Genoa in only five days this time, and we boarded the steamer at night and they locked the hatch doors on us after we had paid every cent of the money in advance and we set sail before dawn. The steamer had been built in 1887." They were at the edge of the beach now and Ruth leaned on Mitchell's shoulder as she put on her shoes. "Nobody can have any idea," Ruth said, as they went up the steps to the concrete walk above, "of what dirt is like, until he has been locked into the hold of a fifty-year-old Greek ship with 700 people for over a month. People died every day and the ship captain would let a rabbi and three other people up on deck at night to perform the burial service and dump the body overboard. The only thing we got to eat was biscuit and canned beef, and there was always worms in everything, even the water we got to drink, and everybody got sores all over their bodies and the old people got too weak to move and the children wept all day, and the relatives of the people who died screamed a good deal of the time, and it is impossible to tell anyone who was not on that boat what it smelled like, in the middle of the summer in the Mediterranean, with a ventilating system that had been installed in Salonika in 1903."

They turned off the beach-walk and climbed slowly up the hill toward the center of the town, past the clean white very modernistic apartment houses with gardens and fountains and balconies that faced the sea.

"We were supposed to be let off in Turkey," Ruth went on, her voice almost without inflection and emotion, as though she were reciting from a ledger the business accounts of an importing firm for the year 1850. "And we had given the Greek money to pay off every officer of the port, but something went wrong and we had to put out to sea again, and we started toward Palestine, although the British had patrols along every mile of coastline. But there was no place else to go. People started to get hallucinations about food, and the sailors would sell a sandwich or a lemon for twenty dollars or a bowl of soup for a gold candlestick. And three of the girls couldn't stand it any more and allowed themselves to be taken up every night to be used by the sailors in exchange for regular meals. It was hard to blame them, but they were cursed by the older people as they walked through the crowd each night toward the ladder, and once a Polish woman with two small daughters knocked one of the girls down with an iron pin and tried to stab her with a kitchen knife she had in her bag."

They turned into Ruth's street and looked up at the window just in time to see the thin edge of light under the blind disappear. They stopped and leaned against a stucco fence in front of a plain, shining white house with cactus plants and a fig tree in the front yard.

"We were on that ship for thirty-five days," Ruth said, "and we came to the coast of Palestine between Haifa and Rehovoth, at night, and maybe someone had been bribed, and maybe it was just lucky, but people were waiting for us in rowboats and in eight hours we were all off. There was one woman, who looked as strong as anyone, a solid, sensible-looking woman, and she seemed cheerful and healthy when she got into the little boat with me, but she suddenly died ten feet off the coast, when the water was so shallow, a child could have stepped out and walked ashore. Luckily, it was a dark night, and there were no patrols, and we were taken in cars to a movie theatre in a little town near Haifa and put inside. The theatre had been playing Betty Grable in 'Campus Confessions,' a musical picture, and there were signs with her in tights and ostrich plumes all over it, and the management had written all over the posters, 'Closed This Week for Repairs.' "

"I saw the picture," Mitchell said. He had seen it one night in Cambridge and he remembered how some of the boys in the audience had whistled when Miss Grable had kissed the leading man.

"We were all told to keep absolutely quiet," Ruth said, "because the British had patrols going through every town. They must have known something, because that week three men high up in the police force were suspended and investigated. It wasn't so hard to keep the older people quiet, but it was awful with the children, and one man really proposed that a little girl who kept crying all day be strangled for the good of the others. We sat there for a week, whispering, making a noise like thousands of mice in a cupboard, and each night cars would come and some people would be taken away to a collective farm somewhere in the hills. Finally, my turn came and I stayed on that farm for two years, working in the fields and teaching children how to read and write German.

"After two years, the British gave you papers, if you managed to dodge them all that time, and I got my papers and started to work for a canning factory outside Tel Aviv. My father was let out of concentration camp in 1938, but his ship was turned back at Haifa, and he was put back in concentration camp in Germany, and for all I know he's still there now, although he's probably dead.

"Joachim wrote me, and my mother, from Berlin. They became good friends once I was gone, and he brought her food, and on Friday nights would come and watch her light the candles. My mother wrote me he told her he had a girl, but he was dissatisfied, he guessed he'd gotten the taste for Jewish girls." Ruth smiled slightly, thinking of the boy with the checkered vest and the monocle many years ago, and Mitchell wondered if he had dropped a bomb near the market-analyzer somewhere in Africa, or in Sicily or Italy.

"He helped my mother get out of Germany," Ruth went on, staring up at the window of her home, which was now secure and dark. "She came out in a Portuguese boat and I heard she was coming and I was on the shore at Haifa Harbor when it came in. But the British wouldn't let it dock, and after six days, they insisted that it turn back, and there were thousands of people on the shore, relatives and friends of the people on the boat, and the worst sound I've ever heard in the world was the sound those people on the shore made when the boat turned around and started to steam toward the Haifa breakwater. But the boat never got out of the harbor." Ruth paused and licked her lips, and spoke very matter of factly. "There was an explosion. We saw the puff of dirty black smoke first, then a long time later we heard the noise, and people on shore were screaming and laughing and crying. Then there was fire and the boat started to go down, and everybody grabbed at any kind of boat they could find and started out toward the steamer, and there were people who couldn't find boats who just jumped into the water, clothes and all, and started to swim, and nobody ever found out how many people drowned that way, because bodies were washed into shore for three weeks afterward. My mother was drowned and five hundred other people on the boat, but 700 were saved and then the British had to let them in, and I suppose that's what the people who set the bomb figured would happen. Some people would die, but some would be saved. If the boat went back to Europe, everybody would be killed. Of course, they bungled it somewhat, and they didn't figure on the fire, and they thought the boat would sink more slowly and only a few people would be killed, but even so it was a pretty fair bargain." Ruth lit a cigarette calmly and held the light for Mitchell. "My mother was washed up a week later, and at least her grave is in Palestine. I couldn't tell my father she was dead, so when I wrote to him in concentration camp, I forged letters from my mother, because I had a lot of her letters and I learned how to make good copies. Even now, through the Red Cross, I write him notes in my mother's handwriting and if he's alive he thinks my mother is living on a farm with a family near Rehovoth."

Ruth pulled at her cigarette and inhaled deeply and in the increased glow, Mitchell looked at her and thought again as he'd thought so many times before, that it was a wonderful and terrible thing that the human race covered its scars so completely, so that Ruth, standing there, with the torture and smuggling and burning and drowning and hiding and dying behind her, looked, with her lipstick and fluffy, cleverly combed hair, and her soft, fragile print dress, like any one of a thousand girls at a dance in America, with nothing more behind them than a weekly allowance from Father, and two proms a season at New Haven or Cambridge.

"Ah," Ruth said, throwing her cigarette away, "she must be asleep by now. Come." She smiled at him, dry-eyed and pleasant, and took his hand, and they walked quietly up through the dim hallways to the apartment in which she lived. She opened the door silently and waved him in, her finger to her lips, and when they were safely in her room, with the door locked behind them, she giggled like a child who has pulled some sly trick on the grownup world, then kissed him hungrily in the dark room, and whispered, "Mitchell, Mitchell," making the name somehow foreign and tender by the way she said it.

He held her tight, but she pulled away. "Not yet, Lieutenant," she said, grinning, "not yet." She put on a light and went over to a chest of drawers in a corner and started to rummage under some scarves. "I have something for you. Sit down and wait, like a polite boy."

Mitchell sat on the low daybed, blinking in the light. The room was small and painted white and very clean. There was a large piece of Egyptian batik in red and dark green on the wall over the bed and there were three photographs on a dressing table. Mitchell looked at the photographs—a round, smiling woman, with a healthy, simple face, Ruth's mother, the picture taken long before the morning when the ship went down in Haifa Harbor. The other two photographs were of men. There was a man who looked like Ruth, obviously her father, a studious, humorous, rather weak face, with frail, delicate bones and shy, childish eyes. And there was the young man in the checkered vest, slender and laughing and proud of himself, with the monocle in his eye like a burlesque of a German general or a British actor.

"Here." Ruth came over to him and sat down beside him. She had a soft chamois bag and there was a little rich clinking as she put it in his hand. "To take with you," she said.

Mitchell slowly opened the bag. A heavy silver medal on a chain, glittering dully in the lamplight, fell into his hand. Ruth was crouched on her knees on the couch beside him, looking anxiously at his face to see if her present would meet with favor. Mitchell turned it over. It was a Saint Christopher, old and irregular, of heavy silver, with the Saint awkward and angular and archaic and very religious in the loving workmanship of a silversmith who had died a long time before.

"It's for voyages," Ruth said, hurriedly. "For a navigator, I thought, it might be quite—quite useful. . . ." She smiled uncertainly at him. "Of course," she said, "it is not in my religion, but I don't think it would do any harm to give it to you. That's why I went to Jerusalem. Something like this, something holy, might have a tendency to be more effective if it comes from Jerusalem, don't you think?"

"Of course," Mitchell said. "It's bound to be."

"Will you wear it?" Ruth glanced quickly and shyly at him, sitting there, dangling the medal on its chain.

"All the time," Mitchell said. "Day and night, every mission, every jeep-ride, year in, year out."

"May I put it on for you?"

Mitchell opened his collar and gave the medal to Ruth. She stood up and he bowed his head and she slipped it on, then leaned over and kissed the back of his neck where the chain lay against the flesh.

She stepped back. "Now," she said matter of factly. "There we are." She went over to the lamp. "We don't need this any more." She put the light out and went over to the window and threw back the blackout blinds, and a faint breeze carrying salt and the scent of gardens came into the room. She stood at the window, looking out, and Mitchell got up and crossed over to her, feeling the unfamiliar cool jewelry of the medal dangling against his chest. He stood behind her, silently, holding her lightly, looking out over the city. The white buildings shone in the heavy moonlight machined and modern and Biblical all at once, and from the west came the faint sound of the sea. Mitchell wanted to tell her that he would remember her, remember everything about her, her drowned mother and imprisoned father, her old, courageous lover, drinking champagne with her at the Nazi cafés; he wanted to tell her that he would remember the dealings with the Greek sailor and the hold of the ship that had been built in 1887 and the dying Jews buying a lemon with a gold candlestick; he wanted to tell her that flying over the Germans in Europe or watching the first snow fall at Stowe he would remember the small boat grating on the sand in the darkness outside Rehovoth and the week in the closed movie theatre with the British patrols outside; he wanted to tell her that the terror and courage would not be forgotten, but he didn't know how to say it, and besides, being honest with himself, he knew it would be difficult to remember, and finally, back in Vermont, it would blur and cloud over and seem unreal as a story in a child's book, read many years ago and now almost forgotten. He held her more tightly, but he said nothing.

"There he is," Ruth said, her voice casual and unimpressed. "See him standing down there next to the house with the picket gate. . . ."

Mitchell looked over Ruth's shoulder. Down on the street, thirty yards from the entrance of Ruth's house, was a small dark figure, almost completely lost in shadow.

"Ali Khazen," Ruth said. "He comes and waits outside my window. Ah . . ." she sighed, "I suppose finally he'll kill me."

She turned away from the window and led him back to the couch across the strip of moonlight that divided the room. She looked up at him gravely, then suddenly pushed him gently down to the couch and fell beside him, holding onto him. She held him and kissed his cheek and chuckled a little. "Now, Lieutenant," she said, "tell me about Vermont."

THE VETERANS REFLECT

The bells were ringing everywhere and the engineer blew the locomotive whistle over and over as they roared up the springtime valley. The hills rolled back from the blue river, and the frail green of the young leaves made them look as though pale green velvet cloth, thready and worn, had been thrown as drapery over their winter sides.

Peter Wylie sat at the window staring dreamily out at the Hudson Valley rolling sweetly and familiarly past him. He smiled when a little girl in front of a farmhouse gravely waved an American flag at the speeding train, and the engineer gravely saluted her in return with a deep roar of the whistle.

Peter Wylie sat at the window of the speeding train and avoided listening to the booming voice of the gentleman talking to the pretty woman across the aisle. He stretched his legs comfortably and half-closed his eyes as he watched the green, quiet country over which, faintly, between towns, came the pealing of bells, because that morning the war had ended.

". . . Dead two years," the gentleman was saying. "His ship went down off Alaska and that was the last we heard of him. Twenty-one years old. Here's his picture, in uniform."

"He looks so young," the woman said.

"He had a blond beard. Hardly had to shave. The ship went down in eighteen minutes . . ."

The bells were ringing, Peter thought, and the graves were full of young men who had hardly had to shave, in uniform. His two cousins on his mother's side, killed in Africa, and Martin, who had been his roommate for three years, killed in India, and all the boys from the squadron . . . The graves on the plains and the mountains, the shallow graves on the hard coral islands, and the long well-kept cemetery of the military dead outside the hospital which you looked at through the tall window of your ward as nurses whispered outside in the corridor, and the doctors hurried fatefully by on their crepe soles. "Convenient," you said with a slow, remote wave of your hand and with what you hoped was a smile, to the nurse, who seemed always to have come from behind a screen where she wept continuously when not actually needed at a bedside. "Modern design."

"What?" the red-eyed nurse had asked blankly.

You had been too tired to explain and merely closed your eyes with the beautiful rudeness of the dying. But you hadn't died. There was a strange platter-like excavation in your abdomen and you would never really enjoy your food any more, and you would always have to climb stairs slowly even though you were only twenty-nine now on this day when the bells were ringing, but the cemetery and the military dead were still there, and here you were on a train up the Hudson Valley on your way home to see your wife and child, and the guns were quiet and the airplanes idled in the hangars, and the pilots sat around and played cards and tried to remember the telephone numbers of the girls in their home towns.

You were on your way home to see your wife and child. For three years, alone at night, sleepless in strange rooms on other continents; on leave, at a bar, sleepless, drinking and laughing, and the brassy old juke boxes playing songs that cried *far away and long ago, far away and long ago,* and all the women being earnest about the war and patriotically anxious to jump into bed with all the pilots, navigators, bombardiers, flight-sergeants, wing-commanders, meteorologists, radio-operators of the air forces of all the United Nations, including the Russian; for three years on the long droning flights across the hundred-mile ripples of the Pacific; for three years, even sometimes at the moment when the bombardier said, "OK, I'll take it from here," as the plane ducked in over the target and the anti-aircraft fire bloomed roughly about you, the faces of your wife and daughter slid through your mind, the woman's firm-boned jaw, the moody blue eyes, the wide, full mouth, familiar, loving, changing, merry, tragic, tenderly and laughingly mocking in the secret, wifely, female understanding of the beloved weaknesses of the man of the family —and the child's face, small, unformed, known only from photographs sent across the oceans, looking out at him through the night with sober, infant gravity. Three years, he thought, and tomorrow morning the train will pull into the dirty old station at Chicago and there they'll be, standing in the soot and clangor, hand in hand, the quick, delightful woman and the fat child, picking his uniform out among the other uniforms, with three years' waiting and loving and hoping showing in the faces as he strode down the platform. . . .

"Bong-bong!" shouted a little bald man, who was leading two women drunkenly down the aisle toward the diner. "Bong-bong. We did it!"

"Ding-a-ling! Ring out the wild bells!" The blonde woman right behind the bald man cried out. "Welcome to America!"

"We applied the crusher," the bald man told the crowded

car. "The old steel spring technique. Coil back, coil back, coil back, then . . ."

They disappeared around the bend of the car over which the small sign said modestly, "Women."

Across the ocean, in the mountains of another country, a man strode out of a darkened house to the long, armored automobile waiting on the night-deserted road. Two men, bundled in army greatcoats, hurried behind him, their boots sighing softly in the damp earth of the courtyard. The chauffeur had the door open, but the man stopped and turned around before he got in and looked at the dark shapes of the mountains rising behind him against the starry sky. He put his hand uncertainly to his collar and pulled at it and took a deep breath. The two men in the greatcoats waited, without looking up, shadowed by the slowly fluttering young foliage of the oaks that bordered the path. The man turned and slowly got into the car, carefully, like an old man who has fallen recently and remembers that his bones are brittle and mend slowly. The other two men sprang into the front seat, and the chauffeur slammed the rear door and ran around to the front and leaped in and started the motor. The automobile sped quietly down the dark road, the noise of its going making a private and faraway *whoosh* that died on the huge and growing darkness of the mountain-circled spring night.

In the back of the car, the man sat bolt upright, his eyes narrow and unseeing, staring straight ahead of him. Off in the hills a church bell pealed and pealed again and again, musical and lonely in the echoing darkness. The lips of the man in the back seat curled slightly, bitterly, as the sound of the pealing village bell wavered on the wind. Germans! he thought. Five million German dead all over the world and the Russians on the road to Berlin and everything worse than 1918 and their leader skulking through the night on backroads toward the Swiss border with a chauffeur and two frightened first-lieutenants and they ring bells as though this was the day after the Fall of France! Germans! Idiots! Imitation suits, imitation rubber, imitation eggs, finally imitation men . . . What was a man expected to do with material like that? And he'd come so close—so close . . . The gates of Moscow. But he sat. The statue sat. Everyone else ran, the diplomats, the newspapermen, the government, and Stalin sat there and the people sat . . . Peasant. Sitting there in his burning house with his gun and his plow—and somehow the house didn't burn. Storm-troopers, assault-guards, blitzkrieg veterans at the gates of Moscow and they died. A little cold and they dropped like hot-house violets. So close—so close . . .

The bell rang more strongly and in other villages other bells answered.

They'd hang him if they caught him. He'd cried at the last Armistice, he'd hang at this. . . . The British use a silk rope when they hang nobility. They wouldn't use silk on him. . . . And the bells ringing all around him . . .

He leaned forward and jabbed the chauffeur fiercely in the back.

"Faster!"

The car spurted forward.

"Production," the booming gentleman across the aisle was saying to the pretty woman, who was leaning closer to him, prettily attentive. "It was inevitable. American production won this war."

Peter thought of the graves, of the English and Chinese and Australians and Russians and Serbs and Greeks and Americans who filled them, who had fought bitterly with rifle and cannon and plane across the torn fields and stripped forests where they now quietly lay, under the illusion that if the war was to be won, it was to be won by them, standing there, hot gun in hand, with the shells dropping around them and the scream of the planes overhead and the tanks roaring at them at fifty miles an hour. . . .

"I know," the gentleman was saying. "I was in Washington from 1941 right to the finish and I saw. I'm in machine tools and I had my hand on the pulse of production and I know what I'm talking about. We performed miracles."

"I'm sure," the pretty woman murmured. "I'm absolutely sure." She was not as young as she had looked at first, Peter noticed, and her clothes were much shabbier than he had thought, and she looked pretty and impressed and tired and ready to be invited to dinner.

". . . Plants in seven states," the man was saying. "We expanded four hundred per cent. The war's over now, I can talk freely. . . ."

The war's over, Peter thought deliciously, settling deeper into his chair, and letting his head rumble pleasantly with the click of the wheels as he leaned back against the cushion, the war's over and machine-tool manufacturers who expanded four hundred per cent can talk freely to women in Pullman cars and tomorrow I see my wife and child and I never have to climb into an airplane again. From now on I walk down to the station and buy a ticket when I want to go some place and I sit down with a magazine and a whisky and soda and the train clicks along on steel and solid gravel and the only enemy activity will be an occasional small boy throwing a rock hopefully at the bright windows of the diner flashing by. Tomorrow afternoon he would be walking slowly along the lake front in the spring wind, hand in hand with his wife and child. "And that, darling, is Lake Michigan. Do you know the water you took a bath in this morning? It comes right from here, especially for you. When your father was a boy he used to stand here and watch the red Indians sail by in their war canoes at forty miles an hour, reciting Henry Wadsworth Longfellow at the top of their voices. I can see by the look in your mother's eye that she doesn't believe me and wants an ice-cream soda. I can also see by the look in her eye that she doesn't think you should have an ice-cream soda so soon after lunch, but I've been thinking about buying you this ice-cream soda for three years and the war's over, and I don't think she's going to make too much of a fuss. . . ."

And tomorrow night, they would lie, soft on their backs in the soft bed, staring idly up at the dark ceiling, his arm under her head, their voices murmuring and mingling with the distant quiet night sounds of the sleeping city, the clack and rumble from the lakefront railroad yards and the soft whisper of automobiles on the highway. . . . "I slept in the same bed in Cairo, Egypt, with a boy from Texas who weighed two hundred and thirty pounds. He wanted to get in the Navy, but he was six feet six inches tall and they said he wouldn't fit on any ship afloat or building. Also he was in love with a girl he met in New York who sold gloves in Saks and he talked about her all night long. She has a thirty-six inch bust and she lives with four girls from Vassar in Greenwich Village and she has a scar on her right buttock six inches long that she got when she fell down iceskating and a man with racing skates ran over her. This is an improvement over sleeping with a two-hundred-and-thirty-pound Texan in the same bed in Cairo, Egypt. Yes, I'll kiss you if you want . . ."

And her voice, close to his ear, in the gentle, tumbled darkness, alive with the fresh night wind off the lake and the familiar smell of her perfume and the frail dry smell of her hair, remembered all the years deep in his nostrils. ". . . And she went to the nursery school in Tucson all day while I was on duty in the hospital and they all liked her very much but she had a habit of hitting the other little boys and girls with her shovel and I had to leave her with my sister. I knew you'd laugh. Stop laughing or I'll stuff a pillow in your mouth, Mr. Veteran. You can afford to laugh, out flying around ten thousand miles away with nothing to worry about but Japs and Germans. Wait till you're a mother and seven young mothers descend upon you to tell you your child has swiped at their children with a wooden shovel every day of the school term . . ." And the kiss to stop the laughter and her head under his chin after that and the slow, diminishing chuckles together for the child sleeping in the next room dreaming of other children and more wooden shovels.

And again, her hand thrown softly and possessively on his chest. "There's a lot more hair here than I remember."

"War. I always put on a lot of hair on my chest in a war. Any objections?"

"No. I'm well-known as a woman who's partial to hairy men. Or is talk like that too vulgar for young soldiers? Am I too fat? I put on eight pounds since 1942. . . . Have you noticed?"

"I'm noticing now."

"Too fat?"

"Ummmmmnnn . . ."

"Tell the truth."

"Ummnnn."

"I'm going to diet. . . ."

"You just wait here and I'll go down and get you a plate of mashed potatoes. . . ."

"Oh, shut up! Oh, darling, darling, I'm glad you're home . . ."

Or perhaps they wouldn't talk at all in the beginning. Perhaps they would just touch each other's hand and weep cheek to cheek for the three years behind them and the years ahead and cling to each other desperately through the long cool night and go to his parents' farm in Wisconsin and walk hand in hand in morning sunlight slowly over the greening fields, their feet sinking into the soft loam, content in the first hours with love and silence, until finally they could sit under the wide peaceful sky, off to themselves, with the rich smell of the newly plowed fields and the watermelon-cucumber smell of the river in their nostrils, and then, finally, the words would come . . . The things he had thought on the long flights, the decisions and doubts of the thousand wartime nights, the deep, deep hallelujah of his spirit as the train covered the sweet final miles between the war and home. He would tell her the things he had had to bury deep within him through the noisy, bleeding years . . . The times he had been afraid . . . The first time he had seen an enemy squadron small against the horizon, harmless-looking dots, growing nearer and larger with insane speed, and the ridiculous way it made him see, over and over again, for some reason, *Acrobatics,* as it was printed in the March Field Bulletin. And at the time he had been shot, six hours away from base, on a rough day, lying bleeding on his parachute while Dennis pushed the bomber toward home, and he had managed to keep quiet for the first four hours, but had wept for the last two hours, almost mechanically, although he had felt very calm. And because he was certain he was going to die, he had for the first time permitted himself to think about whether the whole thing was worth it or not, as the plane bucked in the cold air. He could tell her how he had thought, in those long six hours, of all the boys who had lightly roared off at four hundred miles an hour and lightly and thoughtlessly, or at least silently died. . . . He would be able to tell her that he had soberly decided, bullet in his belly and sure of death in the roaring plane, that it was worth it, that if he had it to do again he would leave home, wife, child, father, mother, country, and search the German bullet out of the cloud once more, part of the enormous anguish and enormous courage of all the men on sea and beach and mountain locked with him in final struggle against the general enemy. And, then, weeping, on the edge of death, as he thought, he could let himself go . . . and for the first time, in the mist of pain, break down the barrier of reserve that had kept him, even in his most secret thoughts, from admitting even to himself how much he loved all those men behind guns—his friends, boys from the same schools, coldly diving, cannons and machine guns tearing out of their wings, at enemy bombers; the pleasant Englishmen foolishly and desperately confident of their ships, sailing formally and arrogantly into hopeless battle like Englishmen in books; the quilted Chinese rifleman standing forlornly on the brown China earth against tanks and artillery; and huge, muffled Russians, fighting by day and night and snow and rain, implacably and ingeniously and tirelessly killing, oblivious to agony or doubt, intent only on burning and crippling and starving and murdering the enemy. . . . He could tell her how deep inside him he had loved all those bloody, weary, cruel, reliable men, how he had felt borne up on that huge tide of men careless of death, and had felt himself to be a part of that tide, agonized, stricken, familiar with defeat, often falsely and frivolously led, but better than the leaders, dangerous, brawling, indivisible—and how he had felt linked with those men for all their lives and his, closer to them even though he could not speak their language nor they his, than to his own mother and father, responsible forever for their comfort and glory as they were for his. And he could tell her of the sober exhilaration of these reflections, this deep dredging to his thoughts, this ultimate examination in the light of pain and exhaustion and terror of himself, who never before this had thought deeply or reflected much beyond the everyday cares of average life in a small town, seated at a desk from nine to five, sleeping comfortable in a quiet room in a warm house, going to the pictures twice a week, playing tennis on Sunday, worrying about whether the car was good for another year or not . . .

The long automobile sped down the winding road among the hills on its way through the night to the Swiss border. The man still sat bolt upright on the back seat, his eyes narrow and unseeing, straight ahead of him.

Victories, he thought, how many victories can a man be expected to win? Paris, Rotterdam, Singapore, Athens, Kiev, Warsaw—and still they kept coming. . . . There was a certain limit to the number of victories that were humanly possible. Napoleon discovered, too . . . Napoleon . . . Napoleon . . . He was tired of that name. In the last days he had ordered that it was not to be spoken in his presence. And now they were all hunting for him, like a world full of bloodhounds—Germans, English, Russians, Americans, French, Austrians, Poles, Dutch, Bulgarians, Serbs, Italians . . . Well, they had reason. Fools. For a long time it hadn't been hard. The cities fell like rotten apples. But then America and Russia . . . The timing was not quite exact. In politics everything happened before schedule. In war everything happened behind schedule . . . So close, so close . . . The Russians . . . Everything else being equal, the bells would be ringing for another reason tonight if not for the Russians . . . Just that winter had to be the coldest in fifty years. There has to be a certain element of luck. Well, all things considered, he had had a successful career. He had started out as a nobody, with his father always yelling at him that he'd never amount to anything and he never could hold a job . . . Today his name was known in every home on the face of the earth, in every jungle . . . Thirty million people had died earlier than they expected because of him and hundreds of cities were leveled to the ground because of him and the entire wealth of all nations of the earth had been strained by him, mines and factories and farms . . . All things considered, he had had a successful career. Even his father would have to admit that. Though, to be fair, if he hadn't grabbed first, someone else would have grabbed. The thing would have happened without him. He had to admit that. But he had grabbed first and the name known in every home on the face of the earth was Hitler, not any other name. So close, so close . . . A little cold and they died . . . Idiots! And now they wanted to hang him. If he could only get across the border, lie low . . . Until the rest of them got tired of killing the Germans. After all, Napoleon came back off Elba. A hundred days. With a little luck he could have stuck . . . Napoleon . . . The name was not to be mentioned. They were going to start worrying about the Russians very soon. The Russians, the Russians . . . The armies had been cut up, they had died by the millions . . . And yet, today they were on the road to Berlin. They were going to need someone to stop the Russians and if he could only lie low for a few months, his name would be mentioned . . . And once he got back, there'd be no more mistakes. With a little luck . . .

The man on the rear seat relaxed against the cushions and a little smile played around the raw mouth.

"I was interviewed by the Washington *Post*," the booming gentleman was saying, his voice cutting into Peter's reverie. "Right before I left. And I told them straight up and down —production must not stop." Peter looked absently at the booming gentleman. He was a tall fat man with a bald head, but somehow he reminded Peter of all the teacher's pets who had ever been in his classes in grammar school—pink, fat face, small, round, pink, satisfied mouth, always impressing everyone with how much he knew and how much in favor he was. Peter closed his eyes and imagined the tall, fat man in an Eton collar with a bow tie and grinned. "Stop a machine for a day," the man was saying, "and industrial obsolescence comes a month nearer. Whether we like it or not we are geared to wartime production."

"You're so right," the pretty woman murmured. Peter looked at her closely for the first time. Her clothes were shabby and she had the same wornout, rundown look that the whole country seemed to have, as though the war had rubbed people and things down to the grain, as though the war had kept the whole continent up too many nights, working too hard . . .

Teacher's pet was bright and shining, as though he had stepped out of 1941 into a world many years older . . .

"Nobody ever had too many guns. I told them right to their faces."

"You're so right," the pretty woman murmured.

"My son was sunk off Alaska . . ." Peter tightened as he recognized the note of boasting in the voice, as though the man were saying he had been elected to an exclusive club. "My son was sunk off Alaska, and I produced machine tools twenty-four hours a day, seven days a week and I have a right to talk. We got it on our hands, I told them, and we have to face the problem fair and square, what are we going to do with them . . ."

"Yes," murmured the pretty woman, hoping for dinner, over the rumble of the wheels.

He would walk slowly, Peter thought, in the evening, after dinner in the big farm kitchen, with the smell of cooking rich and fragrant in the warm kitchen air and his mother red-faced and aproned and his father tall and scrubbed and quiet, smoking his nickel cigar . . . He would walk slowly along the rutted wagon road with Laura beside him in the bright twilight, full of the warm knowledge that he was in no hurry to get any place, that he could leisurely regard the small hills, accepting the night, and leisurely listen to the last evening concert of the birds, leisurely scuff his shoes in the light country dust of the road over which armored tread had never passed, which had never known blood. He could tell Laura finally that of all the good things that had happened to him in this savage, ecstatic century, the best had happened in the moment when he had walked toward her on a train platform in Chicago the day after the war was over. He could tell her finally how tired he was, how tired he had been when bone and blood and nerve had collapsed, when no effort had ever seemed possible again, when his body had given up all knowledge of victory or defeat. And when somehow planes had to be flown and guns manned and swift, deadly action taken by that sodden bone and blood and nerve . . . And somehow the action taken because of the feeling deep within him that on other fields and in other skies, wearier and more desperate men were still manning guns for him and flying more dangerous skies . . . And the promise he made to himself that when it was over and he was home, surrounded by care and love, he was never going to hurry again, never knowingly perform a violent act, never even raise his voice except in laughter and song, never argue with anyone about anything . . . He wasn't going back to his job. Nine to five in a bank at a desk was no way to crown a career of bloodshed thirty thousand feet over three continents. Perhaps Laura would be able to suggest something for him to do, something quiet and unhurried and thoughtless . . . But first he was going to do nothing. Just wander around the farm and teach the baby how to spell and listen to his father explain his particular reasons for rotating his crops in his own particular way. Maybe two, three, five months, a year of that, as long as it took to drain off the blood and weariness, as long as it took for his crippled spirit to open the door of its wartime hospital and step out firmly—as long as it took . . .

"The job's just begun," the booming gentleman was saying. "Let them ring the bells. It amuses them. But tomorrow morning . . ."

"Yes," said the pretty woman, eager to agree with everything.

"We've got to face the facts. A businessman faces the facts. What are the facts? The Russians are near Berlin. Right?"

"Yes," said the woman, "of course."

"Berlin. Fine. Unavoidable. The Russians are sitting on Europe . . ."

Peter tried to close his eyes, close his ears, go back to the dear dream of the twilight country road and his wife's hand in his and the dust that had never known blood. But the man's voice tore through and he couldn't help but listen.

"As a businessman I tell you it's an impossible situation." The man's voice grew louder. "Intolerable. And the sooner we realize it, the better. The truth is, maybe it's a good thing this war was fought. Dramatizes the real problem. Makes the American people see what the real danger is. And what's the answer? Production! Guns and more guns! I don't care what those Communists in Washington say, I say the war has just begun."

Peter stood up wearily and went over to the booming gentleman. "Get out of here," he said as quietly as he could. "Get out of here and keep quiet or I'll kill you."

The booming gentleman looked up at him, his face still with surprise. His little red mouth opened twice and closed silently. His pale eyes stared harshly and searchingly at Peter's worn, bitter face. Then he shrugged, stood up, put out his arm for the lady.

"Come," he said, "we might as well eat."

The pretty woman stood up and started hesitantly, frightenedly, toward the door.

"If it weren't for your uniform," the booming man said loudly, "I'd have you arrested. Armistice or no Armistice."

"Get out of here," Peter said.

The booming gentleman turned and walked swiftly after the woman and they disappeared toward the diner. Peter sat down, conscious of every eye in the car on him, regretting that he had found his next years' work placed so soon before him and crying so urgently to be done. Well, he comforted himself, at least I don't have to travel for this one.

The engineer blew his whistle on a ten-mile stretch of clear track because the war was over and as the hoarse, triumphant sound floated back, Peter closed his eyes and tried to think of his wife and child waiting in the noisy station in Chicago. . . .

ACT OF FAITH

"Present it in a pitiful light," Olson was saying, as they picked their way through the mud toward the orderly room tent. "Three combat-scarred veterans, who fought their way from Omaha Beach to—what was the name of the town we fought our way to?"

"Konigstein," Seeger said.

"Konigstein." Olson lifted his right foot heavily out of a puddle and stared admiringly at the three pounds of mud clinging to his overshoe. "The backbone of the army. The noncommissioned officer. We deserve better of our country. Mention our decorations in passing."

"What decorations should I mention?" Seeger asked. "The marksman's medal?"

"Never quite made it," Olson said. "I had a cross-eyed scorer at the butts. Mention the bronze star, the silver star, the Croix de Guerre, with palms, the unit citation, the Congressional Medal of Honor."

"I'll mention them all." Seeger grinned. "You don't think the CO'll notice that we haven't won most of them, do you?"

"Gad, sir," Olson said with dignity, "do you think that one Southern military gentleman will dare doubt the word of another Southern military gentleman in the hour of victory?"

"I come from Ohio," Seeger said.

"Welch comes from Kansas," Olson said, coolly staring down

a second lieutenant who was passing. The lieutenant made a nervous little jerk with his hand as though he expected a salute, then kept it rigid, as a slight superior smile of scorn twisted at the corner of Olson's mouth. The lieutenant dropped his eyes and splashed on through the mud. "You've heard of Kansas," Olson said. "Magnolia-scented Kansas."

"Of course," said Seeger. "I'm no fool."

"Do your duty by your men, Sergeant." Olson stopped to wipe the rain off his face and lectured him. "Highest ranking noncom present took the initiative and saved his comrades, at great personal risk, above and beyond the call of you-know-what, in the best traditions of the American army."

"I will throw myself in the breach," Seeger said.

"Welch and I can't ask more," said Olson, approvingly.

They walked heavily through the mud on the streets between the rows of tents. The camp stretched drearily over the Rheims plain, with the rain beating on the sagging tents. The division had been there over three weeks by now, waiting to be shipped home, and all the meager diversions of the neighborhood had been sampled and exhausted, and there was an air of watchful suspicion and impatience with the military life hanging over the camp now, and there was even reputed to be a staff sergeant in C Company who was laying odds they would not get back to America before July Fourth.

"I'm redeployable," Olson sang. "It's so enjoyable . . ." It was a jingle he had composed to no recognizable melody in the early days after the victory in Europe, when he had added up his points and found they only came to 63. "Tokyo, wait for me . . ."

They were going to be discharged as soon as they got back to the States, but Olson persisted in singing the song, occasionally adding a mournful stanza about dengue fever and brown girls with venereal disease. He was a short, round boy who had been flunked out of air cadets' school and transferred to the infantry, but whose spirits had not been damaged in the process. He had a high, childish voice, and a pretty baby face. He was very good-natured, and had a girl waiting for him at the University of California, where he intended to finish his course at government expense when he got out of the army, and he was just the type who is killed off early and predictably and sadly in motion pictures about the war, but he had gone through four campaigns and six major battles without a scratch.

Seeger was a large, lanky boy, with a big nose, who had been wounded at Saint Lô, but had come back to his outfit in the Siegfried Line, quite unchanged. He was cheerful and dependable and he knew his business and had broken in five or six second lieutenants who had been killed or wounded and the CO had tried to get him commissioned in the field, but the war had ended while the paperwork was being fumbled over at headquarters.

They reached the door of the orderly tent and stopped. "Be brave, Sergeant," Olson said. "Welch and I are depending on you."

"OK," Seeger said, and went in.

The tent had the dank, army-canvas smell that had been so much a part of Seeger's life in the past three years. The company clerk was reading a July, 1945, issue of the *Buffalo Courier-Express,* which had just reached him, and Captain Taney, the company CO was seated at a sawbuck table he used as a desk, writing a letter to his wife, his lips pursed with effort. He was a small, fussy man, with sandy hair that was falling out. While the fighting had been going on, he had been lean and tense and his small voice had been cold and full of authority. But now he had relaxed, and a little pot belly was creeping up under his belt and he kept the top button of his trousers open when he could do it without too public loss of dignity. During the war Seeger had thought of him as a natural soldier, tireless, fanatic about detail, aggressive, severely anxious to kill Germans. But in the past few months Seeger had seen him relapsing gradually and pleasantly into a small-town wholesale hardware merchant, which he had been before the war, sedentary and a little shy, and, as he had once told Seeger, worried, here in the bleak champagne fields of France, about his daughter, who had just turned twelve and had a tendency to go after the boys and had been caught by her mother kissing a fifteen-year-old neighbor in the hammock after school.

"Hello, Seeger," he said, returning the salute in a mild, offhand gesture. "What's on your mind?"

"Am I disturbing you, sir?"

"Oh, no. Just writing a letter to my wife. You married, Seeger?" He peered at the tall boy standing before him.

"No, sir."

"It's very difficult," Taney sighed, pushing dissatisfiedly at the letter before him. "My wife complains I don't tell her I love her often enough. Been married fifteen years. You'd think she'd know by now." He smiled at Seeger. "I thought you were going to Paris," he said. "I signed the passes yesterday."

"That's what I came to see you about, sir."

"I suppose something's wrong with the passes." Taney spoke resignedly, like a man who has never quite got the hang of army regulations and has had requisitions, furloughs, requests for courts-martial returned for correction in a baffling flood.

"No, sir," Seeger said. "The passes're fine. They start tomorrow. Well, it's just . . ." He looked around at the company clerk, who was on the sports page.

"This confidential?" Taney asked.

"If you don't mind, sir."

"Johnny," Taney said to the clerk, "go stand in the rain some place."

"Yes, sir," the clerk said, and slowly got up and walked out.

Taney looked shrewdly at Seeger, spoke in a secret whisper. "You pick up anything?" he asked.

Seeger grinned. "No sir, haven't had my hands on a girl since Strasbourg."

"Ah, that's good." Taney leaned back, relieved, happy he didn't have to cope with the disapproval of the Medical Corps.

"It's—well," said Seeger, embarrassed, "it's hard to say—but it's money."

Taney shook his head sadly. "I know."

"We haven't been paid for three months, sir, and . . ."

"Damn it!" Taney stood up and shouted furiously. "I would like to take every bloody chair-warming old lady in the Finance Department and wring their necks."

The clerk stuck his head into the tent. "Anything wrong? You call for me, sir?"

"No," Taney shouted. "Get out of here."

The clerk ducked out.

Taney sat down again. "I suppose," he said, in a more normal voice, "they have their problems. Outfits being broken up, being moved all over the place. But it is rugged."

"It wouldn't be so bad," Seeger said. "But we're going to Paris tomorrow. Olson, Welch and myself. And you need money in Paris."

"Don't I know it." Taney wagged his head. "Do you know

what I paid for a bottle of champagne on the Place Pigalle in September . . . ?" He paused significantly. "I won't tell you. You won't have any respect for me the rest of your life."

Seeger laughed. "Hanging," he said, "is too good for the guy who thought up the rate of exchange."

"I don't care if I never see another franc as long as I live." Taney waved his letter in the air, although it had been dry for a long time.

There was silence in the tent and Seeger swallowed a little embarrassedly, watching the CO wave the flimsy sheet of paper in regular sweeping movements. "Sir," he said, "the truth is, I've come to borrow some money for Welch, Olson and myself. We'll pay it back out of the first pay we get, and that can't be too long from now. If you don't want to give it to us, just tell me and I'll understand and get the hell out of here. We don't like to ask, but you might just as well be dead as be in Paris broke."

Taney stopped waving his letter and put it down thoughtfully. He peered at it, wrinkling his brow, looking like an aged bookkeeper in the single gloomy light that hung in the middle of the tent.

"Just say the word, Captain," Seeger said, "and I'll blow . . ."

"Stay where you are, son," said Taney. He dug in his shirt pocket and took out a worn, sweat-stained wallet. He looked at it for a moment. "Alligator," he said, with automatic, absent pride. "My wife sent it to me when we were in England. Pounds don't fit in it. However . . ." He opened it and took out all the contents. There was a small pile of francs on the table in front of him. He counted them. "Four hundred francs," he said. "Eight bucks."

"Excuse me," Seeger said humbly. "I shouldn't have asked."

"Delighted," Taney said vigorously. "Absolutely delighted." He started dividing the francs into two piles. "Truth is, Seeger, most of my money goes home in allotments. And the truth is, I lost eleven hundred francs in a poker game three nights ago, and I ought to be ashamed of myself. Here . . ." he shoved one pile toward Seeger. "Two hundred francs."

Seeger looked down at the frayed, meretricious paper, which always seemed to him like stage money, anyway. "No, sir," he said, "I can't take it."

"Take it," Taney said. "That's a direct order."

Seeger slowly picked up the money, not looking at Taney. "Some time, sir," he said, "after we get out, you have to come over to my house and you and my father and my brother and I'll go on a real drunk."

"I regard that," Taney said, gravely, "as a solemn commitment."

They smiled at each other and Seeger started out.

"Have a drink for me," said Taney, "at the Café de la Paix. A small drink." He was sitting down to write his wife he loved her when Seeger went out of the tent.

Olson fell into step with Seeger and they walked silently through the mud between the tents.

"Well, *mon vieux*?" Olson said finally.

"Two hundred francs," said Seeger.

Olson groaned. "Two hundred francs! We won't be able to pinch a whore's behind on the Boulevard des Capucines for two hundred francs. That miserable, penny-loving Yankee!"

"He only had four hundred," Seeger said.

"I revise my opinion," said Olson.

They walked disconsolately and heavily back toward their tent.

Olson spoke only once before they got there. "These raincoats," he said, patting his. "Most ingenious invention of the war. Highest saturation point of any modern fabric. Collect more water per square inch, and hold it, than any material known to man. All hail the quartermaster!"

Welch was waiting at the entrance of their tent. He was standing there peering excitedly and short-sightedly out at the rain through his glasses, looking angry and tough, like a big-city hack-driver, individual and incorruptible even in the ten-million colored uniform. Every time Seeger came upon Welch unexpectedly, he couldn't help smiling at the belligerent stance, the harsh stare through the steel-rimmed GI glasses, which had nothing at all to do with the way Welch really was. "It's a family inheritance," Welch had once explained. "My whole family stands as though we were getting ready to rap a drunk with a beer glass. Even my old lady." Welch had six brothers, all devout, according to Welch, and Seeger from time to time idly pictured them standing in a row, on Sunday mornings in church, seemingly on the verge of general violence, amid the hushed Latin and Sabbath millinery.

"How much?" Welch asked loudly.

"Don't make us laugh," Olson said, pushing past him into the tent.

"What do you think I could get from the French for my combat jacket?" Seeger said. He went into the tent and lay down on his cot.

Welch followed them in and stood between the two of them, a superior smile on his face. "Boys," he said, "on a man's errand."

"I can just see us now," Olson murmured, lying on his cot with his hands clasped behind his head, "painting Montmartre red. Please bring on the naked dancing girls. Four bucks worth."

"I am not worried," Welch announced.

"Get out of here." Olson turned over on his stomach.

"I know where we can put our hands on sixty-five bucks." Welch looked triumphantly first at Olson, then at Seeger.

Olson turned over slowly and sat up. "I'll kill you," he said, "if you're kidding."

"While you guys are wasting your time," Welch said, "fooling around with the infantry, I used my head. I went into Reems and used my head."

"Rance," Olson said automatically. He had had two years of French in college and he felt, now that the war was over, that he had to introduce his friends to some of his culture.

"I got to talking to a captain in the air force," Welch said eagerly. "A little fat old paddle-footed captain that never got higher off the ground than the second floor of Com Z headquarters, and he told me that what he would admire to do more than anything else is take home a nice shiny German Luger pistol with him to show to the boys back in Pacific Grove, California."

Silence fell on the tent and Welch and Olson looked tentatively at Seeger.

"Sixty-five bucks for a Luger, these days," Olson said, "is a very good figure."

"They've been sellin' for as low as thirty-five," said Welch hesitantly. "I'll bet," he said to Seeger, "you could sell yours now and buy another one back when you got some dough, and make a clear twenty-five on the deal."

Seeger didn't say anything. He had killed the owner of the Luger, an enormous SS major, in Coblenz, behind some paper bales in a warehouse, and the major had fired at Seeger three times with it, once nicking his helmet, before Seeger hit him in the face at twenty feet. Seeger had kept the Luger, a long, heavy, well-balanced gun, very carefully since then, lugging it with him, hiding it at the bottom of his bedroll, oiling it three times a week, avoiding all opportunities of selling it, although he had been offered as much as a hundred dollars for it and several times eighty and ninety, while the war was still on, before German weapons became a glut on the market.

"Well," said Welch, "there's no hurry. I told the captain I'd see him tonight around 8 o'clock in front of the Lion D'Or Hotel. You got five hours to make up your mind. Plenty of time."

"Me," said Olson, after a pause. "I won't say anything."

Seeger looked reflectively at his feet and the other two men avoided looking at him. Welch dug in his pocket. "I forgot," he said. "I picked up a letter for you." He handed it to Seeger.

"Thanks," Seeger said. He opened it absently, thinking about the Luger.

"Me," said Olson, "I won't say a bloody word. I'm just going to lie here and think about that nice fat air force captain."

Seeger grinned a little at him and went to the tent opening to read the letter in the light. The letter was from his father, and even from one glance at the handwriting, scrawly and hurried and spotted, so different from his father's usual steady, handsome, professorial script, he knew that something was wrong.

"Dear Norman," it read, "sometime in the future, you must forgive me for writing this letter. But I have been holding this in so long, and there is no one here I can talk to, and because of your brother's condition I must pretend to be cheerful and optimistic all the time at home, both with him and your mother, who has never been the same since Leonard was killed. You're the oldest now, and although I know we've never talked very seriously about anything before, you have been through a great deal by now, and I imagine you must have matured considerably, and you've seen so many different places and people . . . Norman, I need help. While the war was on and you were fighting, I kept this to myself. It wouldn't have been fair to burden you with this. But now the war is over, and I no longer feel I can stand up under this alone. And you will have to face it some time when you get home, if you haven't faced it already, and perhaps we can help each other by facing it together . . ."

"I'm redeployable," Olson was singing softly, on his cot. "It's so enjoyable, In the Pelilu mud, With the tropical crud . . ." He fell silent after his burst of song.

Seeger blinked his eyes, at the entrance to the tent, in the wan rainy light, and went on reading his father's letter, on the stiff white stationery with the University letterhead in polite engraving at the top of each page.

"I've been feeling this coming on for a long time," the letter continued, "but it wasn't until last Sunday morning that something happened to make me feel it in its full force. I don't know how much you've guessed about the reason for Jacob's discharge from the Army. It's true he was pretty badly wounded in the leg at Metz, but I've asked around, and I know that men with worse wounds were returned to duty after hospitalization. Jacob got a medical discharge, but I don't think it was for the shrapnel wound in his thigh. He is suffering now from what I suppose you call combat fatigue, and he is subject to fits of depression and hallucinations. Your mother and I thought that as time went by and the war and the army receded, he would grow better. Instead, he is growing worse. Last Sunday morning when I came down into the living room from upstairs he was crouched in his old uniform, next to the window, peering out . . ."

"What the hell," Olson was saying, "if we don't get the sixty-five bucks we can always go to the Louvre. I understand the Mona Lisa is back."

"I asked Jacob what he was doing," the letter went on. "He didn't turn around. 'I'm observing,' he said. 'V-1's and V-2's. Buzz-bombs and rockets. They're coming in by the hundreds.' I tried to reason with him and he told me to crouch and save myself from flying glass. To humor him I got down on the floor beside him and tried to tell him the war was over, that we were in Ohio, 4,000 miles away from the nearest spot where bombs had fallen, that America had never been touched. He wouldn't listen. 'These're the new rocket bombs,' he said, 'for the Jews.' "

"Did you ever hear of the Pantheon?" Olson asked loudly.

"No," said Welch.

"It's free."

"I'll go," said Welch.

Seeger shook his head a little and blinked his eyes before he went back to the letter.

"After that," his father went on, "Jacob seemed to forget about the bombs from time to time, but he kept saying that the mobs were coming up the street armed with bazookas and Browning Automatic rifles. He mumbled incoherently a good deal of the time and kept walking back and forth saying, 'What's the situation? Do you know what the situation is?' And he told me he wasn't worried about himself, he was a soldier and he expected to be killed, but he was worried about Mother and myself and Leonard and you. He seemed to forget that Leonard was dead. I tried to calm him and get him back to bed before your mother came down, but he refused and wanted to set out immediately to rejoin his division. It was all terribly disjointed and at one time he took the ribbon he got for winning the Bronze star and threw it in the fireplace, then he got down on his hands and knees and picked it out of the ashes and made me pin it on him again, and he kept repeating, 'This is when they are coming for the Jews.' "

"The next war I'm in," said Olson, "they don't get me under the rank of colonel."

It had stopped raining by now and Seeger folded the unfinished letter and went outside. He walked slowly down to the end of the company street, and facing out across the empty, soaked French fields, scarred and neglected by various armies, he stopped and opened the letter again.

"I don't know what Jacob went through in the army," his father wrote, "that has done this to him. He never talks to me about the war and he refuses to go to a psychoanalyst, and from time to time he is his own bouncing, cheerful self, playing in tennis tournaments and going around with a large group of girls. But he has devoured all the concentration camp reports, and I have found him weeping when the newspapers reported that a hundred Jews were killed in Tripoli some time ago.

"The terrible thing is, Norman, that I find myself coming to believe that it is not neurotic for a Jew to behave like this today. Perhaps Jacob is the normal one, and I, going about my business, teaching economics in a quiet classroom, pretending to understand that the world is comprehensible and orderly, am really the mad one. I ask you once more to forgive me for writing you a letter like this, so different from any letter or any conversation I've ever had with you. But it is crowding me, too. I do not see rockets and bombs, but I see other things.

"Wherever you go these days—restaurants, hotels, clubs, trains, you seem to hear talk about the Jews, mean, hateful murderous talk. Whatever page you turn to in the newspapers you seem to find an article about Jews being killed somewhere on the face of the globe. And there are large, influential newspapers and well-known columnists who each day are growing more and more outspoken and more popular. The day that Roosevelt died I heard a drunken man yelling outside a bar, 'Finally, they got the Jew out of the White House.' And some of the people who heard him merely laughed and nobody stopped him. And on V-E Day, in celebration, hoodlums in Los Angeles savagely beat a Jewish writer. It's difficult to know what to do, whom to fight, where to look for allies.

"Three months ago, for example, I stopped my Thursday night poker game, after playing with the same men for over ten years. John Reilly happened to say that the Jews were getting rich out of this war, and when I demanded an apology, he refused, and when I looked around at the faces of the men who had been my friends for so long, I could see they were not with me. And when I left the house no one said good night to me. I know the poison was spreading from Germany before the war and during it, but I had not realized it had come so close.

"And in my economics class, I find myself idiotically hedging in my lectures. I discover that I am loathe to praise any liberal writer or any liberal act and find myself somehow annoyed and frightened to see an article of criticism of existing abuses signed by a Jewish name. And I hate to see Jewish names on important committees, and hate to read of Jews fighting for the poor, the oppressed, the cheated and hungry. Somehow, even in a country where my family has lived a hundred years, the enemy has won this subtle victory over me—he has made me disfranchise myself from honest causes by calling them foreign, Communist, using Jewish names connected with them as ammunition against them.

"And, most hateful of all, I find myself looking for Jewish names in the casualty lists and secretly being glad when I discover them there, to prove that there at least, among the dead and wounded, we belong. Three times, thanks to you and your brothers, I have found our name there, and, may God forgive me, at the expense of your blood and your brother's life, through my tears, I have felt that same twitch of satisfaction . . .

"When I read the newspapers and see another story that Jews are still being killed in Poland, or Jews are requesting that they be given back their homes in France, or that they be allowed to enter some country where they will not be murdered, I am annoyed with them, I feel they are boring the rest of the world with their problems, they are making demands upon the rest of the world by being killed, they are disturbing everyone by being hungry and asking for the return of their property. If we could all fall through the crust of the earth and vanish in one hour, with our heroes and poets and prophets and martyrs, perhaps we would be doing the memory of the Jewish race a service. . . .

"This is how I feel today, son. I need some help. You've been to the war, you've fought and killed men, you've seen the people of other countries. Maybe you understand things that I don't understand. Maybe you see some hope somewhere. Help me. Your loving father."

Seeger folded the letter slowly, not seeing what he was doing because the tears were burning his eyes. He walked slowly and aimlessly across the dead autumn grass of the empty field, away from the camp.

He tried to wipe away his tears, because with his eyes full and dark, he kept seeing his father and brother crouched in the old-fashioned living room in Ohio and hearing his brother, dressed in the old, discarded uniform, saying, "These're the new rocket bombs. For the Jews."

He sighed, looking out over the bleak, wasted land. Now, he thought, now I have to think about it. He felt a slight, unreasonable twinge of anger at his father for presenting him with the necessity of thinking about it. The army was good about serious problems. While you were fighting, you were too busy and frightened and weary to think about anything, and at other times you were relaxing, putting your brain on a shelf, postponing everything to that impossible time of clarity and beauty after the war. Well, now, here was the impossible, clear, beautiful time, and here was his father, demanding that he think. There are all sorts of Jews, he thought, there are the sort whose every waking moment is ridden by the knowledge of Jewishness, who see signs against the Jew in every smile on a streetcar, every whisper, who see pogroms in every newspaper article, threats in every change of the weather, scorn in every handshake, death behind each closed door. He had not been like that. He was young, he was big and healthy and easy-going and people of all kinds had seemed to like him all his life, in the army and out. In America, especially, what was going on in Europe had seemed remote, unreal, unrelated to him. The chanting, bearded old men burning in the Nazi furnaces, and the dark-eyed women screaming prayers in Polish and Russian and German as they were pushed naked into the gas chambers had seemed as shadowy and almost as unrelated to him as he trotted out onto the Stadium field for a football game, as they must have been to the men named O'Dwyer and Wickersham and Poole who played in the line beside him.

They had seemed more related in Europe. Again and again in the towns that had been taken back from the Germans, gaunt, gray-faced men had stopped him humbly, looking searchingly at him, and had asked, peering at his long, lined, grimy face, under the anonymous helmet, "Are you a Jew?" Sometimes they asked it in English, sometimes French, or Yiddish. He didn't know French or Yiddish, but he learned to recognize the phrase. He had never understood exactly why they had asked the question, since they never demanded anything from him, rarely even could speak to him, until, one day in Strasbourg, a little bent old man and a small, shapeless woman had stopped him, and asked, in English, if he was Jewish.

"Yes," he said, smiling at them.

The two old people had smiled widely, like children. "Look," the old man had said to his wife. "A young American soldier. A Jew. And so large and strong." He had touched Seeger's arm reverently with the tips of his fingers, then had touched the Garand he was carrying. "And such a beautiful rifle . . ."

And there, for a moment, although he was not particularly sensitive, Seeger got an inkling of why he had been stopped and questioned by so many before. Here, to these bent, exhausted old people, ravaged of their families, familiar with flight and death for so many years, was a symbol of continuing life. A large young man in the uniform of the liberator, blood, as they thought, of their blood, but not in hiding, not quivering in fear and helplessness, but striding secure and victorious down the street, armed and capable of inflicting terrible destruction on his enemies.

Seeger had kissed the old lady on the cheek and she had wept and the old man had scolded her for it, while shaking Seeger's hand fervently and thankfully before saying good-bye.

And, thinking back on it, it was silly to pretend that, even before his father's letter, he had been like any other American soldier going through the war. When he had stood over the huge dead SS major with the face blown in by his bullets in the warehouse in Coblenz, and taken the pistol from the dead hand, he had tasted a strange little extra flavor of triumph. How many Jews, he'd thought, has this man killed, how fitting it is that I've killed him. Neither Olson nor Welch, who were like his brothers, would have felt that in picking up the Luger, its barrel still hot from the last shots its owner had fired before dying. And he had resolved that he was going to make sure to take this gun back with him to America, and plug it and keep it on his desk at home, as a kind of vague, half-understood sign to himself that justice had once been done and he had been its instrument.

Maybe, he thought, maybe I'd better take it back with me, but not as a memento. Not plugged, but loaded. America by now was a strange country for him. He had been away a long time and he wasn't sure what was waiting for him when he got home. If the mobs were coming down the street toward his house, he was not going to die singing and praying.

When he was taking basic training he'd heard a scrawny, clerklike-looking soldier from Boston talking at the other end of the PX bar, over the watered beer. "The boys at the office," the scratchy voice was saying, "gave me a party before I left.

And they told me one thing. 'Charlie,' they said, 'hold onto your bayonet. We're going to be able to use it when you get back. On the Yids.'"

He hadn't said anything then, because he'd felt it was neither possible nor desirable to fight against every random overheard voice raised against the Jews from one end of the world to another. But again and again, at odd moments, lying on a barracks cot, or stretched out trying to sleep on the floor of a ruined French farmhouse, he had heard that voice, harsh, satisfied, heavy with hate and ignorance, saying above the beery grumble of apprentice soldiers at the bar, "Hold onto your bayonet. . . ."

And the other stories—Jews collected stories of hatred and injustice and inklings of doom like a special, lunatic kind of miser. The story of the naval officer, commander of a small vessel off the Aleutians, who, in the officers' wardroom, had complained that he hated the Jews because it was the Jews who had demanded that the Germans be beaten first and the forces in the Pacific had been starved in consequence. And when one of his junior officers, who had just come aboard, had objected and told the commander that he was a Jew, the commander had risen from the table and said, "Mister, the Constitution of the United States says I have to serve in the same navy with Jews, but it doesn't say I have to eat at the same table with them." In the fogs and the cold, swelling Arctic seas off the Aleutians, in a small boat, subject to sudden, mortal attack at any moment . . .

And the two young combat engineers in an attached company on D Day, when they were lying off the coast right before climbing down into the landing barges. "There's France," one of them had said.

"What's it like?" the second one had asked, peering out across the miles of water toward the smoking coast.

"Like every place else," the first one had answered. "The Jews've made all the dough during the war."

"Shut up!" Seeger had said, helplessly thinking of the dead, destroyed, wandering, starving Jews of France. The engineers had shut up, and they'd climbed down together into the heaving boat, and gone into the beach together.

And the million other stories. Jews, even the most normal, and best adjusted of them, became living treasuries of them, scraps of malice and bloodthirstiness, clever and confusing and cunningly twisted so that every act by every Jew became suspect and blameworthy and hateful. Seeger had heard the stories, and had made an almost conscious effort to forget them. Now, holding his father's letter in his hand, he remembered them all.

He stared unseeingly out in front of him. Maybe, he thought, maybe it would've been better to have been killed in the war, like Leonard. Simpler. Leonard would never have to face a crowd coming for his mother and father. Leonard would not have to listen and collect these hideous, fascinating little stories that made of every Jew a stranger in any town, on any field, on the face of the earth. He had come so close to being killed so many times, it would have been so easy, so neat and final.

Seeger shook his head. It was ridiculous to feel like that, and he was ashamed of himself for the weak moment. At the age of twenty-one, death was not an answer.

"Seeger!" It was Olson's voice. He and Welch had sloshed silently up behind Seeger, standing in the open field. "Seeger, *mon vieux*, what're you doing—grazing?"

Seeger turned slowly to them. "I wanted to read my letter," he said.

Olson looked closely at him. They had been together so long, through so many things, that flickers and hints of expression on each other's faces were recognized and acted upon. "Anything wrong?" Olson asked.

"No," said Seeger. "Nothing much."

"Norman," Welch said, his voice young and solemn. "Norman, we've been talking, Olson and me. We decided—you're pretty attached to that Luger, and maybe—if you—well . . ."

"What he's trying to say," said Olson, "is we withdraw the request. If you want to sell it, OK. If you don't, don't do it for our sake. Honest."

Seeger looked at them, standing there, disreputable and tough and familiar. "I haven't made up my mind yet," he said.

"Anything you decide," Welch said oratorically, "is perfectly all right with us. Perfectly."

They walked aimlessly and silently across the field, away from camp. As they walked, their shoes making a wet, sliding sound in the damp, dead grass, Seeger thought of the time Olson had covered him in the little town outside Cherbourg, when Seeger had been caught going down the side of a street by four Germans with a machine gun on the second story of a house on the corner and Olson had had to stand out in the middle of the street with no cover at all for more than a minute, firing continuously, so that Seeger could get away alive. And he thought of the time outside Saint Lô when he had been wounded and had lain in a minefield for three hours and Welch and Captain Taney had come looking for him in the darkness and had found him and picked him up and run for it, all of them expecting to get blown up any second.

And he thought of all the drinks they'd had together and the long marches and the cold winter together, and all the girls they'd gone out with together, and he thought of his father and brother crouching behind the window in Ohio waiting for the rockets and the crowds armed with Browning Automatic rifles.

"Say," he stopped and stood facing them. "Say, what do you guys think of the Jews?"

Welch and Olson looked at each other, and Olson glanced down at the letter in Seeger's hand.

"Jews?" Olson said finally. "What're they? Welch, you ever hear of the Jews?"

Welch looked thoughtfully at the gray sky. "No," he said. "But remember, I'm an uneducated fellow."

"Sorry, Bud," Olson said, turning to Seeger. "We can't help you. Ask us another question. Maybe we'll do better."

Seeger peered at the faces of his friends. He would have to rely upon them, later on, out of uniform, on their native streets, more than he had ever relied on them on the bullet-swept street and in the dark minefield in France. Welch and Olson stared back at him, troubled, their faces candid and tough and dependable.

"What time," Seeger asked, "did you tell that captain you'd meet him?"

"Eight o'clock," Welch said. "But we don't have to go. If you have any feeling about that gun . . ."

"We'll meet him," Seeger said. "We can use that sixty-five bucks."

"Listen," Olson said, "I know how much you like that gun and I'll feel like a heel if you sell it."

"Forget it," Seeger said, starting to walk again. "What could I use it for in America?"

PS
3537
.H384
A6

1971